A PLUME E

DEAR ZOE

PHILIP BEARD is a writer and attorney in Pittsburgh, where he lives with his wife, Traci, and their three daughters. This is his first novel. His most recent novel is *Lost in the Garden*.

**A Book Sense Pick**
**Selected for the Borders Original Voices Program**
**Chosen as one of *Booklist*'s Best First Novels of the Year**

"Whatever comparisons are drawn, there is no doubt that this book is a gem all its own."            —Bookreporter.com

"[Beard has a] 'perceptive writer's soul' [and he] 'peels away the layers of his protagonist's anguish simply and sensitively.'"
                                                —*Washington Press*

"The whole novel . . . rings with truth. By the end of it, we're meditating on the ideas of loss and redemption, the ways in which personal tragedies get absorbed into larger ones, but never obliterated, never forgotten."        —*The Buffalo News*

"Affecting."                                    —*Entertainment Weekly*

"Lovely . . . moving."                          —*Publishers Weekly*

"In his soulful debut novel . . . Philip Beard does a pitch-perfect impersonation but never sugar-coats the depths of a young girl's despair."            —*Pittsburgh Post-Gazette*

"*Dear Zoe* is an almost flawless novel of self-discovery and re-demption. It is the sort of book that a generation can call 'theirs,' a book that captures the trials of adolescence and the aching numbness of America in the aftermath of 9/11."

—*The Press of Atlantic City*

"*Dear Zoe* is a powerful story, told in an entirely engaging voice, about how a family gathers itself to move through con-fusion and tragedy toward discovering itself."

—Frederick Busch, author of *Girls* and *The Night Inspector*

"Philip Beard's instinct for voice is remarkable, and he writes with a compassion for his characters we can't help but share."

—Lewis Nordan, author of *Wolf Whistle* and
*The Sharpshooter Blues*

"Applause to Philip Beard for giving us Tess DeNunzio—a sweet, wounded, whip-smart survivor—and her irresistible and haunting story, *Dear Zoe*. This book enchants as it jabs you in the gut."

—Daniel Jones, author of *After Lucy*

# Dear Zoe,

# PHILIP BEARD

A PLUME BOOK

PLUME
Published by Penguin Group
Penguin Group (USA) Inc., 375 Hudson Street, New York, New York 10014, U.S.A.
Penguin Group (Canada), 90 Eglinton Avenue East, Suite 700, Toronto, Ontario, Canada
M4P 2Y3 (a division of Pearson Penguin Canada Inc.)
Penguin Books Ltd., 80 Strand, London WC2R 0RL, England
Penguin Ireland, 25 St. Stephen's Green, Dublin 2, Ireland
(a division of Penguin Books Ltd.)
Penguin Group (Australia), 250 Camberwell Road, Camberwell,
Victoria 3124, Australia (a division of Pearson Australia Group Pty. Ltd.)
Penguin Books India Pvt. Ltd., 11 Community Centre,
Panchsheel Park, New Delhi – 110 017, India
Penguin Books (NZ), 67 Apollo Drive, Rosedale, North Shore 0632,
New Zealand (a division of Pearson New Zealand Ltd.)
Penguin Books (South Africa) (Pty.) Ltd., 24 Sturdee Avenue,
Rosebank, Johannesburg 2196, South Africa

Penguin Books Ltd., Registered Offices: 80 Strand, London WC2R 0RL, England

Published by Plume, a member of Penguin Group (USA) Inc.
Previously published in a Viking edition.

First Plume Printing, May 2006
7   9   10   8

Grateful acknowledgment is made for permission to reprint an excerpt from "Sweet
Baby James" words and music by James Taylor. © 1970 (renewed 1998) EMI Blackwood
Music Inc. and Country Road Music Inc. All rights controlled and administered by
EMI Blackwood Music Inc. International copyright secured. Used by permission.

Ⓡ REGISTERED TRADEMARK—MARCA REGISTRADA

The Library of Congress has catalogued the Viking edition as follows:

Beard, Philip, 1963–
    Dear Zoe : a novel / Philip Beard.
        p.  cm.
    ISBN 0-670-03401-0 (hc.)
    ISBN 978-0-452-28740-2 (pbk.)
    1. Teenage girls—Fiction.  2. Sisters—Death—Fiction.  3. Loss (Psychology)—
Fiction.  4. Fathers and daughters—Fiction.  5. Grief—Fiction.  I. Title.

PS3602.E2525D43  2005
813'.6—dc22                     2004057173

Printed in the United States of America
Original hardcover design by Amy C. King

*For all my girls — Traci, Cali, Maddy and Phoebe*

Dear Zoe,

# Naming You

I have memories of you before you were even born. Maybe that's normal for mothers but I doubt big sisters feel that way too often. I just remember sitting around the kitchen table with Mom and Emily (who was barely four at the time) arguing about what your name was going to be and how that somehow made you into a real person before I ever saw your face. Mom asked Em and me for help because she felt like she had this power with names she had to be careful with. Her middle name is Tess and that's what she named me when she had me at only nineteen—"With big hair and big dreams" she says—and I think sometimes she's afraid that's why I'm turning out the way I am, so much like she was when she married my real Dad instead of how she is now with David.

I was five when Mom and David got married, seven when Mom finally got pregnant with Emily, and even I could see that she was becoming a different person, like a real grown-up. She never looked glamorous anymore—just pretty. She stopped wearing eye shadow and she got a blunt cut that made her look like someone from Connecticut. David had gotten Mom to start reading and she couldn't stop. They read every night and when Mom named Em after Emily Dickinson she felt like that's what she got—this quiet, fearful child who clung to her and seemed to be lonely for no good reason from the day she was born. Never mind that everyone was naming their daughters Emily at the time. Mom had a certain kind of Emily in mind while Em grew inside of her and that's what she got. I was already nine by the time Em turned one and I could tell even then that she was smarter than I'd ever be. But Mom knew that life would be hard for Em, or that she'd make it hard for herself, and one child who already seemed to know there was sadness in the world was enough. You were going to have a name that would protect you from that.

I guess we didn't argue so much as we worked at it, Mom, Em and me. Em seemed to know that this was the first important decision of her life and she didn't fidget or anything. She just sat at the kitchen table with us every evening waiting for her turn. We would each suggest a name and it was the other two's job to say why it was a good or bad idea. Like I would say "Megan" and Mom would say that a Megan in her high school class got pregnant her junior year. Then Em would say "Jodi" because that was her best friend's name and I would remind her that the big slobbery dog down the street was named Jodi and so Jodi was out. Or Mom would say, "How about Jessica?" and Em would say that a Jessica in her preschool class eats paste and that would be enough. "Faith" was too religious, Mom said, and might make her prone to self-righteousness. "Hanna," even though it was becoming popular again, was an old woman's name. "Virginia" was a state, not a name, and ugly besides and even if you called her "Ginny" for short that was *another* dog name and you might just as well call her "Trixie" and get it over with.

We settled on "Zoe" for you not so much because we loved the name but because we didn't know anyone else who had it. Mom thought that would make you your own person. Confident, unique, independent. The weird part was it seemed like it worked. From the time you could crawl we called you "Z," not just because of your name but because that was the shape of your life, always darting from one thing to the next. It wasn't like you got bored easily. It was more like you'd see something else that made you even *more* excited than you already were and you just had to go do that other thing right away. We couldn't look away from you for a second.

      &infin;

It wasn't until we were studying family trees one day in school that I learned you and Em were called my "half-sisters," but I could never think of either of you as a half of anything. Mom and David and I always felt kind of pasted together until Em. She shared blood with all of us and made us a real family. She completed some kind of circle and when you came along you fit right inside it. It's different now. Now it feels like we're just the circle with nothing inside.

Even so, I pretty much knew when I went to live with my Dad for a while that it wasn't such a great idea. I love both of my fathers but it's strange sometimes because I don't really love either of them all the way. It's almost like they're one dad split in two. Mom left my Dad when I was only six months old and we met David when I was three, so he's really all I've ever known as far as a live-in dad, but it's still not the same as the real thing. David is the disciplinarian, the one who makes me rub some of the makeup off my face, the one who's saving for my college education. He never got to hold me when I was a baby and he'd never been a dad before he met Mom, so I think he just thought it was his job to make rules. He was totally different with you and Em, holding you all the time, talking to you like you were adults. I'm not mad about it or anything and I still love him, but it just doesn't feel the same when he hugs me as when my Dad does. My real Dad is a mess, but every hug from him feels like he's never going to let go. David always feels like he's trying to figure out when he's supposed to let go.

David likes to write and he wrote a story about me once. At least I guess to him it was about me but he got me all wrong. I mean, the events that happened were sort of like something that happened to me. When I was twelve I had this friend—another stray, Mom would say—who was always getting in trouble. Her dad had left when she was born and her mom had ditched her with her grandparents when she was ten to go out to California chasing some guy. She went through puberty pretty much pissed at the whole world. She was tall and had boobs by the time she was twelve and decided she liked me for some reason. When Mom suggested she didn't want me hanging out with Kasey anymore I called her a snob, but when she got arrested on our porch (where she'd brought three guys she'd met on work-release from the local juvy center) Mom didn't suggest anymore. She told me if she ever saw Kasey or heard her voice on the phone again I might as well get used to my room because she'd be sliding my meals under the door on a tin tray until I graduated from high school. In David's story he makes himself the bad guy and he and I make some connection out of the situation that changes our relationship forever. He sees that I'm not a little girl anymore, that there is real grown-up danger in my world, and I see that he is doing more than making rules for the sake of making my life miserable. I'm sure there was more to it than that. I'm not much of a reader, but that's what I got out of it. Anyway, like I said, he got me all wrong. The girl in the story is totally naive about her friend—even though there are all kinds of warning signs—until the event with the police, and it's only that event that changes everything. I don't think stuff happens like that. Nothing changes everything. I'd been afraid of Kasey for months and if Mom and David had known about some of the crazy stuff she did and tried to get me to do, it would have ended a lot sooner. But I was scared to stop being her friend too. I was *happy* when she was screaming at those cops because I knew I was out. It was the last in a whole series of events that ended our friendship. But nothing changes everything by itself. Even things that seem like they do. Like me missing the bus on what looked like any other September morning until those planes flew into the tallest buildings in the world. Even you dying, that same day, when I was supposed to be watching you. Or go back to the beginning, around the kitchen table. We could have named you anything and it would have all come out the same.

On the news they say that history is going to be separated by what happened before that day and what will happen after it. But they don't know what they're saying to me.

# David & My Dad

David I think is one of those people who's been wise since he was a little kid. He seems like he's always known how to live his life *just so*. I don't think I'll ever be like that. We both try real hard, David and me, but it just misses somehow, sort of like the story he wrote about me. It's not by much, which is why I think we both keep trying so hard, sort of like what Mom says marriage is like. She says it's like a job where you know the end product is worthwhile but sometimes you hate getting up early for it every day.

It's weird how I've lived with him just about my whole life but David is still this shadowy figure for me. Like I said before, I don't think he really knew how to be a dad until Em came along, and by then the way we were with each other was just the way we were. Neither of us has ever said anything but I think we both feel bad about that missed opportunity. I think maybe he wishes he could go back in time and hold me on his lap or rock me before bed or sit on the couch and watch Disney movies with me a thousand times over. But he can't. When I watched him doing all those things with Em and then you, I realized what was missing between us was physical contact. We spent lots of time together but I was just the little kid he played with and felt responsible for, not one he loved, at least not right away. I really believe he was doing his best with me when we all moved in together. He can't help it if his best is better now, or that loving a new daughter can't change how he is with me. So we're something less than father and daughter. It's not tragic or anything. It's just the way it is.

My real Dad is a disaster but he's my real Dad and I feel something for him that I could never feel for David, even if it's pity sometimes. I know I shouldn't feel that way. Pity is something you feel for people who are trying hard but just seem to be unlucky. My Dad's not unlucky and he's never tried very hard. I guess I feel sorry for him because he can't help being that way any more than I can help being obsessed with the way I look. I miss the bus at least once a week changing outfits or retouching my makeup, which makes David insane. He invents a new punishment every few months—grounding me, adding months to when I can get my permit after I turn sixteen, taking away phone and Internet privileges—all kinds of things even I have to admit seem like they should work. He still hasn't figured out that if I'm looking in that mirror and I don't like what I see, even the guys from the Gap commercials couldn't get me out to the bus stop. I have to give him credit, though, because he never stops trying, and he finally did hit on what would have been the perfect punishment if it hadn't been so cruel even Mom wouldn't let him do it. He said, "Tess, the next time you miss the bus, I'm taking away the makeup *itself*." He

said it just like that, "the makeup *itself*," like he'd just discov-
ered the very center of both the problem and the solution,
which he had. Usually Mom didn't interfere when David got it
in his head to "modify my behavior" in some way, she was too
busy with you and Em, but the best thing about Mom being so
young is she still remembers. She got him to stick with the permit thing, which is why I'll be voting before I drive.

My Dad never tries to change me which is one of the reasons I thought it might be good to go live with him for a while
after you died. It's weird. I can't imagine him with Mom at all.
He pours concrete or drives a truck when he feels like working.
Mom takes tennis lessons and volunteers at the hospital two
days a week. They seem like two people who would never meet
in real life. Mom has told me how it happened, how she was
just a kid herself trying to get away from her own mom and
stepdad, that her "transformation" was a long and painful one.
But I can't see her the old way so I can't see her with my Dad.

I have to give Mom credit for never talking bad about him
around me because the older I get the more I can see how he
must have made her insane. Once I turned twelve or so I
started asking more questions about their relationship and she
told me his biggest problem is that he thinks the world owes
him something. He changes jobs every few months and there's
always a story about how the boss promised him this or that
and didn't deliver. Never mind my Dad only worked there for
six months; he thinks he should be the foreman since he knows
more than "all them little shits." Plus I also found out that
whenever he's worked somewhere long enough the county at-
taches his wages because he owes Mom like $15,000 in child
support payments. It's not that he never spends any money on

me. He takes me shopping and buys me clothes and stuff but somehow when it gets taken out of his pay it's not for me but for "them government assholes." The thing is, he seems happy most of the time. One time he was driving a truck for an ice cream company and he dropped off like ten gallons and told Mom it was his support payment for the month. Mom has pretty much given up on that money anyway, so she laughed. David was pissed, of course. He sees my Dad the way the rest of the world sees him and he can't understand why Mom won't go to court to get her money. Mom says the whole thing with my Dad was so much like a different life that she feels out of place when she steps back into it, even to think about something like that. My Dad can't understand why everyone can't just get along. He knows he screwed up in letting Mom go but it's like he also knows he could never have handled the responsibility anyhow and that both of us are better off with him being the guy dropping off ten gallons of ice cream. Which we probably are.

You weren't old enough to appreciate it, but seeing my two dads talking to each other is one of the funniest things ever. You'd think they'd hate each other but it's more like they're in some kind of contest to see who can climb the farthest up the other one's ass. The only time they have to talk is when my Dad comes to pick me up to go somewhere. I used to sleep over at his place at least one night every weekend but my Dad breeds German shepherds to make extra money and after I started getting my period the dog smell made me want to vomit. Also there were a couple of gang-related shootings in his neighborhood, so then we just started going out for brunch or to a movie or to see my Gram or my cousins or something. He has a family the size of a small town. Anyway, do you remember how big my Dad is? David and my Dad are about the same height but David could stand behind him and you'd never know he was there. My Dad lifts weights almost every day of his life, even when he's working construction, and he has to buy all his clothes at a special store. You were even scared of him at first and you weren't scared of anyone, until he started getting down on his knees and calling you "the Big Z." Then you started flirting with him and talking a mile a minute like he was your best friend.

But even though he does stuff like that I don't think Mom has many fond memories of him. One time I asked her why she married him and she told me this story about how she was at a high school football game, up in the stands, and she spotted my Dad coming around the track with two of his weight-lifter buddies. She was supposed to meet him so she starts walking down the grandstand and sees this big group of guys, maybe ten of them, from the other school headed toward my Dad and his friends, and she could tell something was going to happen. She was really scared and started calling to him to look out and my Dad turns around and stops—just starts watching this pack of wolves moving in. By the time Mom is down by the track the two groups are facing each other a few feet apart, like in a movie, and everyone in the stands has stopped watching the game. Someone in the middle of the group from the other school says something like, "You don't look so tough now,

Nicky DeNunzio," and my Dad looks at him and doesn't even blink, Mom says, and he says, "You ain't got enough guys."

Mom wouldn't tell me much about the rest. There was a big fight and some of the guys from the other school got hurt pretty bad before they gave up and ran. She said she was never so scared in her life and that she should've known to stay away from him but when my Dad said that—"You ain't got enough guys"—she fell in love with him and thought he would keep her safe forever. She used the story as an example of how stupid she was, how she found out she was never really safe with him, but I thought it was kind of romantic.

Anyway, that was my Dad in high school. David was in the musicals. In his yearbook pictures he looks like he weighed about 120 pounds. Not that he still looks like that. But he listens to people like Frank Sinatra and Harry Connick, Jr., and James Taylor, and when my Dad comes to pick me up it's like David's back to being the skinny kid who got picked on by guys like him. He's always asking my Dad if he's "goin' liftin'" later, dropping the "g"s like he's always telling me not to do. Or he'll start in on the Steelers, who he couldn't care less about, and end up saying something that even sounds stupid to me, like "You know, Nick, they need to score more touchdowns or they're gonna be in for a long season." But the funniest part is that if they were still in high school my Dad would be dissing David all over the place, but since David is this hot-shot attorney and my Dad is basically a zero in the professional-life department, he's not even hearing how stupid David sounds because he's too busy sounding stupid himself: "Yeah, I think this new gig with the ice cream company is the big one. The boss promised me two months on the road and then he'll promote me to supervisor. If that happens and I can get Zelda and Keisha to drop two litters each this year, I'm movin' outa that shit hole. Yep, this could be the year." Jesus. Sometimes if I already have a friend over she'll come with my Dad and me and then it's all I can do to get us all out the door before David and my Dad start doing the brown-nose boogie right in front of someone who could make or break my entire high school reputation.

# Anniversary

Even though it's been almost a year, sometimes I still miss you so much it feels like someone is pushing their finger into the base of my throat and I cry like it just happened yesterday. But now when I cry like that it kind of feels like it cleans me out, and each time it happens it feels like I'm going to have a little longer until it happens again and usually I do. It's not that I'm missing you less. It's more like I'm finding a place to keep you.

Mom and David are doing okay too, or at least better. When I first came back from my Dad's I think they were so relieved to see me that things were really good for a while. But now sometimes everything gets quiet again, like Emily and I are orphaned sisters living in a fancy old hotel by ourselves except there are these two servants who just happen to also be my Mom and my stepdad to make sure we get to school and get fed, keep the house clean and fix stuff when it breaks. When I was trying to explain to the doctor we all go see together now why I went to live with my Dad, she stopped me after a while and asked if I felt like Mom and David excluded me from their grief. My whole chest started to feel tight and I had to hold my breath for a minute because I never could have thought of that, never put it into those words, but that was it. You died in this tiny, silent part of that day, and by trying to protect me from their sadness Mom and David just helped make that silence continue.

The hardest part is going to be the day itself, the anniversary. The world will stop. People will cry. They will relive the pictures and the familiar video of what to them felt like the beginning of the end of the world. But it will be just like before. You won't be any part of what they're thinking about. You'll just be the silence itself. Every living person, even ones who lost no one, will be thinking of all those people who fell out of the sky and no one except Mom and David and Em and me will be thinking of you. And I will have to feel all the guilt again. Not just the guilt that goes along with remembering that day and you, which is always there, but the guilt that tightens around my chest because I don't care about all those others, because I even resent them for dying on the day that should have been yours alone.

# Less Construction

I think part of the problem with David and me is that I'm not precocious like Em is or you were. I didn't even know what that word meant until I heard David use it to describe you once and I went to look it up because I felt like a moron not understanding something about my own sister. It even took me a while to look it up. That second "c" threw me. My vocabulary sucks and David says that's going to kill me on the SATs. He says the only way to improve my vocabulary is to read something other than *Seventeen* or *Rolling Stone* and to talk to people who don't use "like" as their only adjective. He also suggested that if I spent half the time reading that I spend putting my makeup on or doing my nails or tanning or applying late night masks to my face, Harvard and Yale might hold a lottery to see who gets me. He might have a point but there's nothing I can do about it. David doesn't get that you can't scare someone into being motivated. You either are or you aren't. You can't change what you care about. And it's weird because I never judge other people by how they look. I'm not one of the "popular" kids and none of my friends are going to appear in any Abercrombie ads any time soon. I just can't help it. Whatever self-confidence I have comes from the way I look, or at least the way I think I look.

I write all the time but not for school, nothing anybody would ever want to read. And I like to read, magazines and stuff, those Chicken Soup books, but not the books we read in English, every one of which was written before anyone I know was born. David went to my same high school and I found his name in one of the copies of The Crucible in my English room. That was weird, seeing his name printed there in handwriting that was totally different than his is now but somehow still the same. Anyway, I don't figure I'm going to learn any new words reading something that's been putting high school students to sleep for a thousand years. Maybe I just don't know how to read. We watched the movie of The Crucible after we were done reading it, the one with Winona Ryder crying every twelve seconds and going ape shit all over the screen, and I thought, hey, this is a pretty good story. How did I miss all this? When I'm reading for school, I can see how good the writers are, how they use just the right words, but I don't make any emotional connection somehow. It's kind of like watching soccer. Our team went to States last year and almost every guy on the team was cute but I still couldn't sit through a whole game.

Anyway, David's lectures can be worse than soccer, especially when he gets on an SAT roll, but I know he's just trying to make sure I turn out okay. He doesn't seem as worried about Em and I can see why, I guess. Em is quiet, real small for her age, already a bookworm at eight. It's like he figures she's bound to turn out okay just because she came from him. With me, he knows I came partly from my Dad and I think he figures he's got his work cut out for him.

Every time my Dad picks me up it's in a different car in some state of disintegration. There was the Chevy Nova that you used a screwdriver to crank the window. There was the Honda Civic that had been in about seventeen accidents and even my Dad with all of his muscles had to bash his shoulder against the driver's side door until it opened with a sound like he was bending it in half. He even had a Pinto for a while—that car that was basically outlawed sometime in the eighties because it apparently blew up when someone as much as tailgated you. Inspection is never a problem because he never keeps them long enough to get them inspected. He mostly buys them from friends and then junks them when they stop running.

The worst though was when he started his own construction company and bought an old dump truck. His "company" consisted of him and one other guy who helped him out between AA meetings and they didn't really do real construction, just concrete work. Anyway, he named the company after me, and he had TESS CONSTRUCTION stenciled in huge black letters across the rusted yellow bed of the truck. Both sides. The first time he pulled up in that thing Amy Bregar had slept over and was supposed to come to brunch at King's with Dad and me. We were kind of hanging out in the living room, looking out the big picture window for him. Her eyes got real big when she saw what we'd be riding in and if she wasn't already my best friend she would have moved up to that spot right then because she didn't say a word. Keisha, one of my Dad's German shepherds, was looking out the passenger-side window, and even she looked embarrassed. My Dad had this huge smile on his face when he got down from the cab and he sort of looked back over his shoulder as he walked down the sidewalk to our walkway like he couldn't believe it was really his. Mostly I think he was proud of the stenciling, which even though I guess it did show how much he loved me I wanted to kill him for. He practically skipped up the steps to our porch and I was already at the door trying to make my eyes as slitty as I could.

"I am *not* getting in that thing," I told him. He looked at me like I just told him his mother was ugly. Which she is.

He said, "Whadaya mean? Dontcha see the sign?"

I said, "Yeah, I see it and that's exactly why I'm not getting in."

I could feel David in the hall behind me. He was usually the one who made sure I got off okay with my Dad, instead of Mom, and I thought if he starts in on the ass-kissing small talk with my Dad, especially if he starts telling him how great the new truck looks, I'm maybe going to try to pierce my jugular with my French manicure. But he was holding you and I guess this was back when you were still afraid of my Dad because he kept his distance and stayed quiet at first. My Dad was saying that the name was going to be good luck and that once the business got going he was going to build a house in the empty lot next to my Gram's. But I was standing my ground. I was not getting in that truck. Amy sort of stood off to the side, not really rooting me on, but anyone could see how she wanted this to come out. Then David came up behind me holding you. He got real close and I could smell his Old Spice mixing with your baby lotion, and he sort of whispered in my ear, "Just go, sweetie." It really startled me. He never used the soft-sell with me. He always told me what to do like he was reading it out of a manual that had no exceptions in it. So when he said that, "Just go, sweetie," I didn't know what to do. Everything stopped for a few seconds. It was like this little moment for us, for David and me, and it gathered up all the energy that had been going into arguing with my Dad and sucked it away. I never looked at David and you, and I don't know if he felt it too, felt that moment, or if him talking like that, low and soft, was more for your benefit. I just walked past my Dad and out the door. He held the door for Amy and she followed, like we were both doing exactly what we wanted to be doing. I should have been pissed at David but instead it was like I felt myself loving him a little bit for the first time on my own terms—not because he was my stepdad or because Mom loved him or because he took care of us and kept us safe, not for the things he did, but for once because I could see who he was. Maybe he showed himself that way to me all the time and that was the first day I was old enough to see it, I don't know.

That spell lasted about exactly a minute because then the three of us were jammed into the cab of the truck sitting on a ripped leather seat with Keisha. She was pregnant and another warm body within three feet of her made her hot and start to pant like she'd been trapped in a little doggie tanning bed for about a day and a half. With the three of us taking up the whole seat Keisha had to straddle me to get her head out the window and her tongue was practically dragging on the asphalt. Amy looked straight ahead and tried not to look like she was ducking every time a car passed and I put my head down on Keisha's shoulder and faced out the window. As we pulled out I saw that David had come out onto the porch so you could wave to me. You had this look on your face like you couldn't understand why this big truck was taking me away and when you waved it wasn't your usual big, full-arm flap. You just raised your arm and held it there, like you weren't sure I was ever coming back.

# Roller Coaster

Even though the doctor we're seeing together now did help me understand that one thing, that Mom and David excluded me from their grief, I'm not sure what good talking about stuff with a stranger week after week does for anyone. I guess therapy might be okay for people who don't really know why they're sad or angry or whatever. I'm a simple case. You're gone and I will never be the same. Never. I can talk, I can "share" until there's nothing secret left but you'll still be dead and I'll still be sad. I went to a different doctor by myself right after, but it just made things worse. She tried to be all soothing, like she could make me feel better just with the tone of her voice. Miss Soothing would even ask me, at the end of our sessions—after I'd sat there silent, not talking or even hearing what she was saying until I could sense it was time to go—"Do you feel better?"

Better? What I wanted to ask her, what I would have asked

her if I thought she'd give an answer I could use, was Why shouldn't the loss of someone you love ruin you?

For me what helps is not talking about it, letting time pass. Or talking about it with someone I love, with you. That's my therapy. I think the reason grown-ups think regular therapy works is because time passes while they're in it. They're not really getting better because they're talking about it. They're getting better because time is passing and they're learning to live their lives again because they have to. We have to.

Em is different now, not so fearful, which seems strange to me I guess since I'm more afraid. I remember once just before you were born I was babysitting for Em while Mom and David were at some charity event. I had put Em to bed and I was watching TV and I heard her start to cry. I went into her room and asked her what the matter was and she said, "I'm lonely." But it was spooky because it wasn't like she meant she was lonely just then but all the time. Like she lived her days that way, got through them, but then it all caught up to her at night that she was this little solitary being. It made me so sad I got into bed with her and stayed there until Mom and David woke me up. Mom asked me what happened but I never told her. You had to hear Em say it to know what she meant and I knew there was nothing Mom could do anyway. I mean it wasn't like Em was neglected. This was something different. Not an insecurity Mom or David could have helped her with, but an understanding of who she was and would be. Then again, I was just getting my period and I was totally hormonal so maybe I added a few layers of drama to the whole situation. Maybe she did just want a little company. But I don't think so.

There's something you did just as well to miss. I got my first period when I was eleven. When I was ten Mom started talking to me about it a lot, like we were about to share this wonderful thing, and I couldn't seem to talk or read enough about it. Mom couldn't believe how much there was in the magazines I read compared to when she was a kid and after six months or so I was telling her stuff she didn't know until she was like twenty-five. Anyway, it happened at school during a group presentation in French class, which could have been scary and humiliating except that I knew exactly what was happening and that I was the first one of my friends to get it. Mom left the hospital early to come and get me and after I got cleaned up we went out for a big celebration lunch. I was only eleven years old but it was like this gap closed between us. Even though Mom wasn't quite twenty yet when she had me she still always seemed like all the other moms until that day. It was like all of a sudden our lives got squeezed together. I could have a baby now and be to somebody else what she was to me. It brought us together like nothing else could have and I remember her looking at me across the table that day and starting to cry with this big smile on her face.

That lasted maybe two months until it became clear that I was now only a normal person for like five days a month. Everything else was premenstrual, menstrual or postmenstrual. And Mom and I got synchronized just like I'd read about, so we were like these two parallel lunatics on side-by-side tracks of a racer roller coaster, up and down, up and down, sometimes hugging across the tracks, sometimes trying to send each other falling to our deaths. It wasn't until Mom got pregnant with you that I realized how much I needed her company. It was no fun riding that roller coaster alone let me tell you. You can't get a good fix on anyone when you're the only one moving.

I can tell I'm a pretty sexual person. I think it runs in the family, which is probably why Mom's always worried about me, even though I'm not much of a partier. Grammy was eighteen when she had Mom. Mom was nineteen when she had me. I was always a little boy crazy, even before. But once I got my period it was like there was nothing else in the world. Like they glowed while everything else went gray. My friends and I did nothing but talk about them, fight over them, trail them around the halls like sucker fish on a pod of whales. It was like we needed their blood to survive. But they're *useless*. Let's not even talk about emotionally, since between the ages of eight and seventeen they mature maybe six months. Even physically. Even if you give them what they want, let them up your shirt, down your pants, rub the lump in their jeans and send them home with a wet spot, they can't return the favor. I'm not ashamed to say I've hooked up with a lot of boys from my school and I'm still waiting for one of them to touch me the right way. I've given up on that entirely. I take care of business when I get home, which is just fine. I let three of them touch me "down there," hoping three would be a charm, but when they got there every one of them stopped like they'd just scored their first touchdown but didn't know how to do the little dance. I guess you can't really blame them. Pleasing themselves is as simple as working a butter churn for half a minute. When they're with us, they don't know a) what they're looking for, b) where to find it, or c) what to do if they manage to get there by accident. Three strikes and you're out. I decided after number three gave me a pelvic exam I was going to wait for someone who was worth teaching the little dance to, I didn't care if I was twenty-five.

# My Face

The kind of face I have is the kind that's basically okay but needs some help to look pretty. And since my face is broader, like my Dad's, the hair has to be just right too or I look too much like Arnold from Hey, Arnold. My morning routine is a big issue between me and David, not just because of how much time it takes me but all the treatments and cleansers and makeup and stuff. David says to start saving my money now because someday Health & Beauty is going to be all mine and is *not* included in my college fund. That part I understand but you tell me how I could do it any faster.

My bus comes at seven so I get up at five-thirty, five-twenty if I want to eat something, which I usually don't. I'm not even a little bit of a morning person and pretty much everything tastes like Styrofoam to me before nine. So I get in the shower around five-thirty and that takes about a half an hour, maybe a little more. Right away, that makes David insane. For him everything has one purpose. You use the shower to get clean and that takes a certain short amount of time. He doesn't understand that things can maybe have different purposes for different people. I use the shower to wake up. Sometimes that takes five minutes, sometimes fifteen but there's no way to rush it. You can't make yourself awake.

David's all about efficiency, both time and money. One time he got so exasperated with my time in the shower and what was being spent on Health & Beauty that he made me write out my morning routine exactly, including every step, the time required and the products I needed, so we could get together and see what could be left out or made faster. He tried to get me excited about it by pointing out that maybe I'd get more sleep, but I already knew my routine was something that couldn't be shortened without affecting the end product. Anyway, he said to treat it like something I was writing for public speaking class, something that would not only describe but explain my routine to my "audience." Here's what I gave him:

*Once I've been in the shower long enough to be awake* (avg: 15 minutes) *I make the water cold and shampoo my hair twice* (Herbal Essences - Volume)—*once to get the dirt and oil out and the second time for volume. The cold water keeps your hair from splitting. Then I condition* (also Herbal Essences) *but only from the middle of my hair down. If you condition up near your scalp it gets all oily. At the same time I'm rinsing out the conditioner* (see, I'm conserving time) *I'm scrubbing my face* (St. Ives Apricot Scrub) *and rinsing that, still with cold water to close my pores. I make the water hot again and lather shave gel* (Skintimate, Tropical Splash) *on my legs, shave, rinse, then wash my whole body with my body pouf* (Dove) *and body wash* (Neutrogena Body Clear). *I use the same body wash to lather and shave my underarms because I don't really*

27

need the gel there (see, conserving money). I rinse everything in the hot water, then make it as cold as I can again for about five minutes to close all my pores. That's pretty much it for the shower. I wrap my hair in one towel and my body in another and step out. How can you do all that in less than half an hour?

I comb my wet hair (never brush—brushing breaks wet hair and makes flyaways) for about five minutes, then I dry it on high for ten minutes and on low for another five, add a few curlers for volume and keep those in while doing my makeup. Total makeup time is no more than twenty minutes to do all of the following:

Foundation (Mary Kay) to even skin tone.

Concealer (Cover Girl) on zits, eye circles and creases around the nose.

Eye Shadow (Maybelline, brown), not too much or my step-dad will take his thumb to it.

Eyeliner (Almay Wet and Cover Girl pencil). Wet for on top of the top lid, pencil for underneath the top lid and in the corners.

Mascara (Maybelline) on the top lashes only. Putting it on the bottom makes your eyes look smaller and makes you look Goth besides.

After makeup, the curlers come out and I brush and style, dryer on low, for maybe five minutes tops.

Then it's time to pick the outfit which is no easy thing with the new dress code. Anything that shows cleavage or your belly button is illegal, which means no tank tops and takes out about half my wardrobe, even though I have no cleavage to show. Also, anything sleeveless is out so I can't even wear high-cut, full-length tank tops. No short shorts, no miniskirts, no visible piercings other than ears (not an issue with me since I faint at needles). Usually, I try on three or four things but end up with a three-quarter-sleeve shirt and jeans *with my high-heeled brown sandals. All accessories are silver—hoop or raindrop earrings, big silver rings on five fingers and both thumbs, some with turquoise stones, and a silver beaded necklace.*

That's it. And I know for a fact I'm faster than most of my friends. But David says he's not interested in "relative performance," whatever that means.

*Yours*

Now let me tell you about the kind of face you had.

I have this picture of you and Mom on my desk in my room. You are kneeling on her lap, facing her, and your mouth and eyes are both smiling right at her like there's no one else in the world. In the background, out of focus, is a railing, from a boat or a dock, I can't remember, and then dark blue water. When people see it they say what a great picture it is of the two of you, and they're right. But I don't think any of them notice that you can't see Mom's face. The picture is taken from the side but slightly behind her and the wind has blown her hair so that even her prominent nose is hidden. It's a picture of Mom's hair and your face. But without knowing it everyone sees Mom's face in yours. That's the kind of face you had. The kind that reflected the world and made it beautiful.

# Banana Slippers

Just because I thought about killing myself once doesn't mean I'm someone people should feel sorry for. It wasn't one of those drama things, right after you died. At first there was the funeral and the memorial service, which were awful, but there were all these people around, people who really cared about you and about us, and they created this energy that, even though it came out of sadness, sort of kept you alive for those few days. But then everyone left and there just seemed to be these endless moments without you. I was sadder than I ever thought a person could be. Until the next day when it was worse. And then the next and the next. It wasn't so much like falling into a deep dark hole as it was like being forced to climb down a ladder along the steep sides. Every day some force pushed me down another couple of rungs and the rungs I had just come from disappeared so there was no way out. At first it was really scary, going down like that. Then the sadness started to gather weight and I started to welcome it, started trying to gather it up. It seemed like there was nothing else so I wanted as much of it as I could carry with me. And the whole time I'm going down like that I can't stop thinking about how everything is so random but so connected, how everything seems like it's both a total matter of chance and predetermined at the same time. What if I didn't miss the bus that day? What if the weather hadn't been so perfect that we decided to stay outside? What if the car hadn't rounded the corner and started down our street just after the first tower came down? Or what if the towers never came down at all? That could have happened. If the plane that hit the Pentagon had been the first one? Cell phone calls might've been made to the passengers headed for the Trade Center, like the people who went down in Pennsylvania. Maybe there's a struggle, the planes go down in Brooklyn. Different people would be dead, you might be alive. Who am I to wish for something like that? Or keep going back. What if Mom hadn't been strong enough to leave my Dad? Or even if she was, what if we'd never met David? I mean we met him in a *grocery* store for godsake. Who knows where we'd be living? Probably with my Dad and his dogs and I'd have other, different little sisters, maybe a brother, and Em wouldn't be lonely, wouldn't *be* at all, and you never would have even been alive so you could die. But it all *did* happen, one after the other, and everything led to that day, like that car hitting you was a picture pasted to a domino that had been waiting its turn to fall my whole life. Further back in the line there was another domino, David smelling a cantaloupe, smiling at Mom. It was crazy. The only order that made sense was me going down that ladder, and it started to feel really good. Then one day it seemed like I reached the bottom. I stayed there for at least a week, not going to school, not getting out of bed. Without the movement, without the ladder down, there was nothing. Mom made me go to that doctor again, the one I'd refused to see anymore, but it didn't matter who I saw because even sitting in her office I was sitting at the bottom of my hole. A voice outside me told her what I knew she wanted to hear. Mom and Miss Soothing whispered for a while afterward and we stopped at the drugstore on the way home. I wanted to move again, to go down deeper. I thought, maybe the medicine, before bed. I went to the bathroom cabinet. Mom had hidden mine but not hers, the pills she took to help her sleep. It should have felt melodramatic, looking at a bottle of sleeping pills, like a bad movie, but I didn't feel like I was trying to do something to myself. I just felt like I was trying to get somewhere. I wanted darkness so deep and dense I could feel it against my skin, holding me. Even the little night-light in the bathroom was blinding and I squinted at the label to keep it out: ELEANOR GLADSTONE, TAKE ONE TABLET BY MOUTH AT BEDTIME AS NEEDED.

Something about seeing Mom's name made me stop for a few seconds. It wasn't that I was reconsidering. Being there didn't feel like a decision in the first place. I didn't have that level of control. It just stopped feeling like opening the bottle was the next thing that was supposed to happen. Mom needed these, not me. The label even said so. Then Em appeared in the doorway of the bathroom. She was wearing those big yellow banana slippers, the ones you used to try to walk in. Remember? You'd lift one foot as high as you could, then the other, like you had canoes on your feet. I put the bottle back in the medicine cabinet and closed the door. She said, "What're you doing?" I told her, "Nothing. Go back to bed." But she just stood there in those stupid slippers, looking at me, not blinking for the longest time. Her thin blond hair was stuck to one side of her face and her little nightie slid off one of her narrow shoulders. "You first," she said.

Can you believe that? She knew. Or she knew something. And looking at her face, I felt like I was seeing her as the adult she would be twenty or thirty years from now and I could tell that she would be someone I would listen to. So I did. She didn't move when I walked past, and I remember deciding not to touch her on the head.

# New Paint

When you died, there was still both a crib and a bed in your room. You were experimenting with your bed. You were "dabbling," Mom said, and that was okay. At first, you tried the bed only at nap time, and only when Mom put you down. If it was me or David you always wanted your crib. Then you started showing off for us too, getting yourself under the covers and turning your face away when either of us tried to kiss you, like you were too old for that. Mom's only rule was you couldn't change your mind. You couldn't decide on your bed and then come wandering out half an hour later asking for your crib. I heard David complain one night about all of the bedtime negotiations and he said maybe he should take down the crib and put an end to it. Mom just said, "Everything in time."

Which was why I didn't understand why she decided to paint so soon. It was the last day of school before Christmas break and I could smell it as soon as I came through the door. I followed the smell up to your room and looked through the crack in the door. Your bed and your crib and the rest of your furniture were all covered with old sheets. Mom had already done all the edges—along the floorboards and crown molding, around the windows and in all the corners—and now she was starting to roll a deep beige color over the pale yellow sponge painting she and I had done together, over the Peter Rabbit characters she had outlined by hand, for hours and hours, and then let me help with the coloring and shading. And she was crying. Not just a soft crying, but shaking so that I didn't know how she could even see what she was doing.

I sat down outside the door trying to stay quiet, crying too, listening to the sticky sound of the roller erasing what we had done together. Erasing part of your life without ever asking me what I thought, if it was okay to do that yet.

When David came home that night the paint smell was still real strong and he knew right away. Mom was asleep on the couch, exhausted from all of the work and the crying. I was trying to keep Em busy with a game until David could get us a pizza or something because the refrigerator was totally empty. He looked at me and said, "Please tell me she didn't." And when I didn't say anything, he took the stairs two at a time and then I heard the door slam and I felt like I could see him standing in the middle of the room, spinning slowly around, seeing nothing but your brown, flat walls.

He stayed up there a long time and when he came down he went out the front door quietly without saying anything to Em and me. We finished our game and then I made us both peanut butter and jellies. After that, I gave Em a bath and read her a few stories, and then we both went to bed, with David still out and Mom downstairs.

After a while I heard Em crying softly so I went in to see what was the matter.

She said, "I can't sleep with that smell."

I said, "Just try. You'll get used to it. It's not like a noise or anything."

She sat up and wiped at her eyes with her sheet. "Yes it is," she said. "When I breathe it in it makes a noise inside my head."

"That's just your imagination, Em."

"No it isn't. Can you sleep with me?"

"Em, the smell's not going to go away just because I'm in here."

"Yes it will. I'll put my face against you."

"Okay."

I got in bed with her and turned on my side so she could snuggle against my back. She fell asleep in about five minutes but I laid there awake for a long time, thinking about what Em said. Because it seemed like she was right. It seemed like when I breathed in, the fumes from the paint made a swishing sound in my head and I remembered that whenever our grass got long you used to take your shoes off and make me swing you back and forth over it, so your bare feet barely touched the tops of the grass. That's where I should have been that day, outside with you the whole time. It was warm enough we could have taken your shoes off. The sound of bare feet brushing grass. That's exactly the sound the new paint made in my head.

I fell asleep to it, and when I woke up it was gone.

# David & Me

It was David who woke me. He said, "Tess, honey. It's time to get ready for school."

He was standing over me and for a second I thought he was going to touch my forehead but he didn't. He was already in a suit and tie. Or maybe it was the same one from the day before, I couldn't remember. Em was sound asleep next to me. She still had another hour or so before she had to get up but David went over to her dresser and started opening and closing drawers, picking out something for her to wear and laying it on top. It took him a while but he finished picking Em's outfit, then he went over to her closet and found her sneakers and set those on her dresser too.

"Tess, are you awake enough for me to go downstairs?"

"Yeah, I think."

"Up 'n' at 'em."

David left and I rolled out of Em's bed, stiff from hardly having any room to move all night. Em never stirred. I went into the bathroom and was about to get in the shower when I realized how hungry I was from the night before, so I went downstairs.

Mom must have moved up to her bed because the couch was empty. When I went into the kitchen David was sitting at the table eating a bowl of cereal and watching CNN. On the screen there was a computer-generated cartoon of a new kind of bomb and someone was explaining how it could blow up caves way down underground. The cartoon showed it doing that and I stood and watched for a while. Then I got myself a bowl and a spoon and sat down.

We both ate quietly for a while. Usually I didn't have anything but orange juice before school because I'm always running late. David would be eating and watching the news, telling me every time I walked through the kitchen what time it was and that I better get a move on. As soon as he was sure I was going to make the bus he left for work. Today he didn't seem to be in as much of a hurry.

I asked him, "Are you putting Em on the bus?"

"I thought I'd let your mother sleep."

He finished his cereal and took his bowl to the sink. I noticed for the first time that his clothes looked big on him. He looked around the room but not like he was looking for anything. It was more like he didn't know what to do with himself and I thought he was just anxious to get to work.

He said, "What time does Em get up?"

"I think around seven-thirty."

"Oh."

He looked at his watch and then at the clock on the oven.

I asked him, "Are you making her a lunch or is she buying?"

"I don't know."

"The menu's over on the frig. She only likes the chicken nuggets, the spaghetti or the pizza. Otherwise she packs."

"Okay. Thanks."

"Peanut butter and jelly."

"Okay."

He made the sandwich and cut the crusts off just when I was about to tell him. He put some chips in a baggie and found an apple in the refrigerator that still looked okay, then started opening cabinets, looking for something.

He asked me, "Does she have a thermos?"

"Give her a juice box."

"Okay. I think I knew that. Geez, I haven't done this since you were little."

"You packed my lunches?"

"Yeah, most of the time. Your mother was still working then and she had to leave before I did. Plus you come by your morning routine honestly."

"Mom?"

"Don't you remember her hair? I think it made her six inches taller."

"I remember. I thought she looked like a model."

"She did. Still does."

I had seen David cry once, the day you died. Never before or since. So when he started just then, without any warning, I didn't know what to do. I looked down at my cereal and waited. He stopped as quickly as he'd started, like the stopping was something he practiced.

Then he said, "I'm sorry."

"That's okay."

"Juice box, right?

"Yeah. Citrus Cooler if we have it. The green."

"Right."

He finished packing her lunch and set it next to her backpack on the counter. He looked like he was about to leave the room but then he opened the drawer under the phone and scribbled something on a Post-it note, unzipped Em's lunch box and stuck the note to the side of the juice box. Then he said thanks a lot for helping him and he went upstairs to wake Em, even though it was still early.

That could have been the beginning of something maybe, if David and I were different people. Instead, it was the beginning of him getting Em up for school every day, getting to work late and coming home even later. So that meant it was also the beginning of me putting Em to bed most nights. In a way we were taking care of Em together, but we were doing it apart. And no one was really taking care of either of us, so we had that in common too. But it wasn't the beginning of what it could have been because David and I weren't very good at being what we could be, just what we were. And after you died, I mean, after what happened that day, it felt like we had no chance anymore.

On my way out of the kitchen I opened Em's lunch box to look at the note he'd written.

It just said, "Have a good day. I love you, Daddy."

*Justin*

After a while, the sleeping pills weren't enough for Mom. The medication they put her on made her foggy and forgetful, not like herself at all, even after they took her off it. She got mad easily at Em when she paid attention to her at all, and she and I seemed to move through the house bouncing off each other without touching or saying much of anything. Covering up your walls didn't help her, or any of us. If anything the house got even quieter, as if the characters Mom had painted over had voices we couldn't hear anymore. David stopped Mom from finishing the redecorating project, so now there was a crib and a little bed and furniture with Peter Rabbit knobs on the drawers in this room that was painted like someone's guest room would be.

Em and I were spending more and more time together. She had always seemed so much older than her age and losing you made her even more like an adult in a little kid's body. Mom fell asleep on the couch by 8:30 every night, before David got home, which is why I started putting Em to bed. Instead of reading stories we'd just talk and sometimes I'd end up sleeping with her. Then, like I said, David got her up and ready for school every morning. That's pretty much how things went until the day I decided to leave.

I want to tell you about that day, but before I do, I want to tell you about another day. It's one of those days that was nothing at the time and only means something because of what happened later.

It was May, I think, four months before the accident. You were almost three. Mom did most of her shopping at the Giant Eagle at the mall but whenever we ran out of milk or eggs or something, one of us would walk toward the river to Marsico's. You loved going because Justin, this young guy who worked there, always gave you a lollipop. Em was playing over at a friend's house and you asked me to come along with you and Mom so I wouldn't be lonely. That cracked me up, so I came.

Did you realize how beautiful Mom was? Is.

I guess all children think their mothers are beautiful. At least for a while, until they get old enough to compare. But if you'd ever gotten old enough you would've found out. A lot of my friends' moms are pretty but they're all a lot older. And some of them aren't all that pretty once you get to know them. You couldn't have known this but there's a lot of money in the area where we live, not so much in our neighborhood but up the hill away from the river, and I swear some of the women look pretty just because of that. It's part of their attitude, like they have enough money that the definition of pretty automatically gets expanded to include them. Mom isn't that kind of pretty.

When I have guys over I catch them staring at her all the time. Some of the guys I've hung out with always want to come over instead of me going over to their houses with their ordinary parents. Part of it is her age but mostly she's just beautiful. And not just in the way that makes strangers look at her longer than they realize but also in that way you never get tired of. I never thought about it when I was a kid but for a couple of years after I got my period it really bothered me. We look enough alike in pictures, but I'm built more like my Dad, square and broad shouldered, straight and flat in all the wrong places, and I got his wide nose instead of Mom's pointy one. My girlfriends who have met her are always telling other girls, "Have you ever seen Tess's mom? She's, like, *gorgeous*." It was really annoying at first but then I actually started to like the effect she had on my guy friends. It was fun to watch them blush and stumble over their words and look sideways when she talked to them, like she was the sun or something. But if I really liked a guy enough to want to go out with him or anything, I tried never to bring him home.

So anyway, we're walking down to Marsico's, you're between Mom and me and we're swinging you down off each curb and up onto the next one and when we get to the corner where Marsico's is you pull away from us and go running through the open door by yourself. Mom and I can hear Mrs. Marsico talking to you before we even get to the entrance. She's one of those people who thinks little children will understand you better if you talk real loud. She's saying, "You're not all by yourself are you sweetheart?" You don't even hear her question. You say, "Can I have a lolly?" Mrs. Marsico laughs at you real loud and she's got both of her big wrinkled hands on your cheeks when we come in. "Oh, there you are," she says. "Let me get Justin." Mom says don't bother, we just need a few things, but Mrs. Marsico kind of winks at her and says Justin will be mad at her the rest of the day if he knows Elly Gladstone came in without him knowing. Mom says, "Oh don't be ridiculous!" but you could see her blushing a little bit.

Justin's a little older than my friends, like maybe he'd be in college if that's what he'd decided to do, but he looks pretty much like my friends do around Mom. She's telling him what we need and he's moving so fast it's like he's trying to keep up with her and get each thing before she says the next one. Like some kind of stock boy shorthand. Which is funny because once he gets it all bagged up he doesn't seem to want us going anywhere. He takes you behind the counter and lifts you up to pick a lollipop from the jar and then he keeps you on his hip while he writes our name and all the items on the receipt for our charge account. He plays this little game with you before writing each item. He says, "Now, let's see. Did you get any hippo lips today?" "No!" you squeal. "How about slug juice?" "No!" "Did you get . . . milk?" "Yes!" Then he bends over the counter and writes "milk" real slow and carefully. We only got like four or five things but it takes him at least ten minutes to get it all down. Frankly, it makes me want to puke. I mean I'm wearing a pink tank top and white shorts and I might as well be invisible. I have to give him some credit, though, because he looks like he's just about as much in love with you as he is with Mom. He's mostly concentrating on you but I can tell you're helping him not look at Mom, and every once in a while after you laugh or say something cute he'll look at her real quick, like he and Mom are your parents and they're sharing in watching you. Or at least that's how he wants to think of it. That first little blush is gone from Mom and now she just looks like she always does. That amazes me about her. I would have given anything for guys, real guys like Justin, to look at me the way they looked at her, but if they did I never could've been that cool about it. When I can tell someone's interested in me I'll flirt with him even if I don't really want to go out with him just to see how far he'll go, what he'll say to get me to like him. But there was Mom, just sort of enjoying her ten minutes of warmth from Justin like she might enjoy the sun on her face on our way home—like she didn't have to give anything back, just accept it into her skin.

What was really weird for me about this little thing with Justin, though, was that about eleven years earlier Mom and I had met David in a grocery store. We'd just moved out of Grammy and Pap's into a small apartment on Center Avenue and Mom and I were at the Giant Eagle stocking up for the first time. I was three, not much older than you were that day at Marsico's, so I don't know if I remember it as clearly as I think I do or if maybe I've just heard the story so many times I think I remember. But I swear I can feel myself on that hard plastic seat in the front of the grocery cart. Mom's looking at her list even though we need just about everything because she loves her lists, and I think now that she particularly loved that list, the first one that was hers and mine alone.

I was a fiend for cantaloupe when I was little. I would eat it as fast as Mom could slice it up and sometimes we'd share a whole one at one sitting. The Giant Eagle must have just gotten a new shipment because from my seat in the cart it seemed like there were cantaloupe stacked to the ceiling. David was there, shaking and smelling them but not looking like he knew why he was doing it. I don't remember not knowing him so in my memory it's like we'd been walking up and down the aisles looking for him. And then there he was, holding the one thing I wanted more than anything else in the store. The way Mom tells it, David very coolly asked her how you went about picking one of these things out, looking more at the cantaloupe than at her, and she never says so but you get the feeling not many guys had ever reacted that way to her. The way David tells it, with body motions and everything, he looked up at Mom and did a Three Stooges double-take and staggered back from the sight of her. I don't remember it either of those ways. I just remember feeling the fact of Mom and me becoming Mom and David and me.

That's one of the strangest parts about being a stepchild. You get to actually watch your parents fall in love and then get comfortable with each other. And what's even weirder is that there isn't any security in that, especially as you get older and see how things can change. People who fall in love can fall out of it. I'm sure it never occurred to you that Mom and David ever "met," or that they could decide not to live together, or decide which one of them you would live with. For you, they were a couple, two parts of a whole. For me, they are a relationship that can end like any other.

Last May, about eight months after you died, I started noticing more and more items from Marsico's in our refrigerator and pantry. They carried brands you never saw at Giant Eagle, Turner's Milk, Hershey's Ice Cream, Monk's Bread. At first I figured it was Mom's new forgetfulness that had her going there more often. Then one day she asked me to walk down and get her some macaroni and cheese for dinner. I asked if it could wait until Em came home from school so she could go with me and Mom said, "Just go!" and fell into the love seat in front of the TV with all her weight.

When Justin saw me he disappeared behind the meat counter, so I asked Mrs. Marsico for the mac and cheese. She wrote up the receipt and bagged it without saying anything. After I had stepped out and crossed the street, Justin came running after me with an envelope in his hand. He looked white and kind of sick, like he had a fever or something. He asked if Mom was home, then asked if I'd mind giving her the bill from last month. He hadn't seen her in a week or so and said it seemed silly to put it in the mail just to go up the street. He didn't let the envelope go when I first reached for it, like he knew he was making a mistake, and I noticed that it didn't have our name and address on it, that it just said "Elly" on the outside.

The house was quiet when I got home. Em still hadn't gotten off the bus and the TV was on but Mom had the volume all the way down. I handed her the bag and stood there holding the envelope, feeling calm in a weird way, like I was the parent. "What's that?" she asked. I said, "You tell me, Mom," and tossed the envelope onto her lap.

She could have said what Justin had said, that it was our last month's bill, maybe even convinced me. But like I said, she wasn't herself anymore.

She said, "It's nothing you need to worry about, Tess."

"Whatever, Mom."

"Tess, believe me. It's nothing."

"Mom, I said it doesn't matter. I think it's great. Really. I didn't think you gave a shit about anyone anymore."

She looked at me hard and I could tell she was going to say something for the first time in her life that was meant to hurt me. She said, "Tess, you can't always get comfort from people who have the same pain you have." She looked down and fingered the envelope before tearing it into small pieces she left sitting in her lap. Then she started to cry and turned her head in a way that told me to leave.

She might have regretted it, saying that to me, and it wasn't really important what exact truth she was telling me about what did or didn't happen between her and Justin. What was important was that I decided she was right. There was no comfort in our house. And all of a sudden you being gone felt like it filled up every room until there wasn't any space left for me.

There were only a few weeks of school left. My Dad wasn't really working then, so I knew he could take me and pick me up every day. More important, I knew he would. I packed a bag and called him. He didn't ask any questions. Except what time did school let out. And did I mind riding in a mail truck.

# The Truck

Every summer my Dad and I would go to Kennywood at least three times. Remember Kennywood? You went a couple of times with Mom and David and me for the school picnic and the last time we went you were old enough to ride in Kiddie Land. I spent an hour or so with you before meeting up with Amy Bregar and a couple of guys and you and I went on the Tea Cups together. You never stopped laughing the entire time. I got that thing spinning so that the other kids in our cup were screaming for me to stop but you just kept laughing harder and harder. The whole world was a blur except for your face.

My Dad lives close to Kennywood, near all the old steel plants that have been shut down, and it was someplace he could take me that was special but without spending too much money. I'm like you, I can ride anything. So Dad and I would stay all day long riding everything two or three times, then break for dinner and ride until it closed at eleven o'clock at night. Back when I was still sleeping over at his house once in a while, we'd leave the park after closing and go to Kings for waffles and bacon, then go to his house and crash until like noon the next day. God I loved that. Even when I was little I loved to sleep, but I almost never got to sleep in like that at home. David's a morning person and can't understand how anyone can waste "the best part of the day" in bed. To me the best part of the day *is* when you're in bed. Anyway, even though I loved going to Kennywood with my Dad he always talked about how he wished he could take me to Disney World. I never begged him to take me there or anything; it just seemed like something he wanted to do. Especially after Mom and David got married. I guess maybe he was afraid he was losing me, plus he saw what a nice neighborhood we moved into and probably figured David was going to beat him to it if he didn't hurry. So when I was in second grade we went down together for spring vacation. It didn't really cost him anything. He'd gotten park tickets from a friend he was doing concrete work for and we drove down in his brother's pickup and stayed at this little motel maybe forty-five minutes from the park. But I wasn't old enough, eight I guess, to care that we were doing everything as cheaply as possible. All I cared about was us being together. Even though I saw him just about every week and talked to him on the phone all the time, the drive down to Florida was about the longest I'd ever spent where I was close enough to touch him the whole time. I remember I didn't even really care that we hardly got to ride anything the first day. I guess that time of year practically every family in the United States is at Disney World. Every ride had waits of like an hour and a half, even the little Dumbo ride that just goes around in a circle and up in the air if you pull back on the handle. They have the exact same ride in Kiddie Land at Kennywood, remember? Except the elephants aren't Dumbo and you can ride it at least thirty times in an hour and a half if you want to. Anyway, I didn't care but I could tell my Dad was getting pretty pissed. We'd gotten in late the night before and slept in that morning, so by the time we got to the park it was so crowded he had to carry me to feel like he wasn't going to lose me. By dinnertime we'd ridden three rides and been to the Hall of Presidents (which was really boring but there was no line). Then it took us an hour to get a couple of hot dogs. While we were eating Dad said he was sure it would be just like Kennywood. Everyone would start taking their kids back to their hotels after dark and that's when we'd have the place to ourselves.

He was wrong, of course. If anything it got more crowded after dark. Someone told us, "Everyone comes back for the parade!" Dad said, "What parade?" and by the time we made our way to a spot where it was supposed to pass we were in a crowd of people at least fifteen deep. Dad said maybe we should go ride while everyone was watching the parade, so we went way back into the park and found the *20,000 Leagues Under the Sea* ride. I'd never even heard of that movie and when David took us back a few years ago that ride had been shut down, but Dad said it would be fun and the wait was only forty-five minutes. When we finally got to the front of the line this whole group of kids in wheelchairs got pushed around all the ropes by their parents and cut right in front of us. It didn't matter. It just meant we had to wait for the next nuclear submarine. But Dad picked me up, pushed past the kid dressed like a Soviet naval officer and found the exit. Then we headed out of the park. I was never one of those kids who cried when it was time to go home but I remember putting my face into the hard muscles at the base of his neck and not looking at anything on the way out, not even Cinderella's castle that I knew changed colors at night.

The next morning the alarm clock in our room went off before it was even light out. Dad told me to go back to sleep and he'd be back as soon as he could. I don't know how long he was gone because I was still sound asleep when he opened the door carrying juice and doughnuts. He showered while I ate and when he came out he said, "You ready for another big day?" I nodded but I was thinking maybe I'd rather stay and swim in the little hotel pool. "How're your legs?" he asked me.

I told him, "Okay, I guess."

He said, "Not tired?"

I said, "Yeah, a little."

He said, "C'mon. Let's go."

Outside the room in the parking lot, sitting in the bed of the pickup, was a dark blue wheelchair.

I said, "What's that, Dad?"

He said, "That's your little chariot, Tess DeNunzio."

I said, "But I'm not crippled." I didn't say that because I thought we were doing anything wrong (though I remember feeling like maybe we were) but just to state the facts.

He said, "And we ain't usin' it 'cause you're crippled. We're usin' it cause your legs are tired. Like a wagon. They are tired, right?"

I said, "Yeah. I guess."

He said, "Well, let's go then."

So we did and Disney World was like the Red Sea for us for the rest of the week. No one seemed to look at us but they moved aside as if they could feel us coming. It was like being famous and invisible at the same time. We rode so much we got tired of riding by the middle of the day, so we'd take the Monorail to one of the fancy hotels near the park, change in the bathroom by the pool and swim all afternoon. I think we went to a different hotel pool every day. Then we'd go back to the park for dinner and ride all night.

The only reason I tell you that story is, since I only see him once a week or so, part of me had never given up feeling like my Dad still had the same powers he had when I was eight. I guess that's what I was expecting, or at least hoping, when I called him after Mom tore up that letter from Justin. For him to pick me up in whatever rusted-out chariot he was driving and rescue me, make me invisible again.

It wasn't exactly a mail truck, not one of those white square things that almost touches the ground, but it was close enough. As far as I could tell it had been a UPS truck, maybe in the seventies, if there even was UPS back then. Someone had painted over the packing-paper brown with lime green and someone else had tried to cover over that mistake with a coat of black. Neither of the top coats had held very well so the effect was a sort of camouflage Partridge Family look. He was late, thank you Mary Mother of God. All the buses had gone. Still, when he pulled up in front of where I was waiting with my gym bag, I felt the opposite of invisible.

He asked me did I like it and I asked him if he was insane.

He said he got a great deal on it and I said I bet he did.

That was pretty much it for the conversation for a while. Even if we'd wanted to talk it was pretty hard to hear once that thing got going more than ten miles an hour. And Dad looked like he needed to concentrate pretty hard to drive. The truck had one of those long stick shifts that comes out of the floor and the steering wheel went from his stomach almost all the way to the windshield. I swear he had to turn that thing 720 degrees just to make the right turn out of the parking lot. Anyway, we stayed quiet and I just watched the trees go by through my window and the road go by through the holes near my feet. For the first time in a long time I wasn't thinking about you. I was thinking more about Mom and about how she was alone now. I mean, I knew she still had David and Em, but since for part of my life it had been just me and Mom, I felt like by leaving I was leaving her alone.

Because of the dogs and the shootings and everything it'd been almost four years since I'd been to my Dad's house and when we turned into his neighborhood I was pretty shocked. I don't know if it had gotten that much worse or if I really didn't notice as much when I was little. The houses were mostly all row houses or so close together they might as well have been. The porches all had those rusted tin awnings, green and white or brown and white, and there was junk on most of them. The sidewalks were all cracked and there was grass growing out of them, especially around the signposts and near the curbs where no one walked. The street was a dead end and way at the end past a fence you could see all these old smokestacks and you'd have thought from looking at it that the plant was abandoned, except there was fire shooting up out of one of them.

My Dad's house looked nicer than the ones around it but not much. He had replaced his concrete steps and his few feet of sidewalk and there were a couple of lawn chairs and flower boxes on his porch. But the nice stuff was what even my Dad would've called "whipped cream on dogshit." You got the feeling these houses weren't even nice when they were new, like whoever built them knew they were just going to be covered with soot and filled with immigrant steelworkers anyway, so why bother. At least back then the soot meant they were part of something. Now the air was clean but the houses stayed dirty.

I jumped down out of the truck with my gym bag and followed my Dad up onto the porch. After he turned about sixteen different locks Zelda and Keisha and Keisha's new litter greeted us at the door, which was pretty fun except the smell was even worse than I remembered it. At least at a kennel or a vet's office the floors are all tile or concrete or something you can clean. At my Dad's house the smell comes up still warm out of the carpet and almost makes you dizzy.

I took my gym bag up to the room where I always used to stay. It was smaller than I remembered but it looked and smelled like it'd just been painted, maybe even the night before. There was a twin bed pushed into one corner and that was the only furniture. The shade on the window was pulled down like always because there was a window from the house next door so close you could lean out and touch it. I never understood why they bothered with the windows.

Dad said, "We can fill it up if you decide to stay a while." He was standing in the doorway behind me. All six puppies had followed him up and their tails were waving real loose. He was holding the phone and he handed it to me. Part of our deal was he'd pick me up without Mom knowing if I called her as soon as we got there. I dialed and the answering machine came on but Mom picked up when she heard my voice.

"Tess, honey, where are you?"

"It's okay, Mom. I'm with Dad. I'm at Dad's."

"Why?"

"I'm going to stay with him for a while."

"You're what?"

"I'm staying with Dad for a while."

"Tess, don't be ridiculous. Your father can't even take care of himself."

"And you can?"

"That's not fair."

"Mom, when did you realize I didn't get off the bus today?"

She didn't say anything and I knew my voice on the phone was the first time she'd even thought of me.

"I just need to be away for a while, that's all."

"Tess, honey, we need to be together, all of us."

"You mean like we've been? You said it yourself, Mom. We can't help each other."

"I didn't mean that."

"Yes you did."

"Tess . . ."

"I'm not trying to be mean, Mom. It's true. We can't even look at each other anymore and it's just getting worse. We're all like ghosts in our own house."

She started to cry and I had promised myself I wasn't going to do that. I needed to keep that day as a new beginning for me. I handed the phone to my Dad.

He said, "Elly, don't worry about her."

Then he said, "Look, she's with me, okay?"

Then he said, "That was different."

He said, "She'll call you tomorrow."

My Dad went back downstairs but the puppies stayed with me which I was surprised about. This one who was the smallest had really blue eyes and a swoop of white fur that came down across one of them like the opposite of a patch. I decided pretty quick that he was my favorite and he must have known it because after I held him for a while he started treating me like his territory. Whenever one of the others would try to hop into my lap he'd get all yappy and start gnawing on an ear with his sharp little teeth. I started calling him Frank because of his eyes and when I heard my Dad pouring food into bowls downstairs all the others went running, but Frank stopped for a second at the door and looked at me like, "Are you coming or what?"

# Church

I slept most of Saturday and so did my Dad. I heard him get up
to let the dogs out into the little fenced-in patch of grass in the
back but then I don't remember anything until I smelled bacon
at around noon.

My Dad loves to cook. He went to school for it for a while
during one of his many brief periods of trying to actually make
something out of his life but when he got to the part of the program where you got to work in a restaurant as sort of an intern,
he quit because he didn't like the "little flaming pussy chef" he
got assigned to. Mostly I think he realized the hours were going
to suck. Anyway, he makes a mean broccoli cheddar soup now,
so that's something. And he's always been great with breakfast.
David eats Raisin Bran every morning of his life, which I guess
is okay when every day of your life starts at six A.M. But at noon
you need meat and syrup-related items. Dad and I ate and
watched TV until early afternoon. Then we played with the
dogs for a while and he showed me how to teach Frank how to

sit by holding some food in front of him and then pushing it back over his head. It was pretty neat how his little bum went right down when his nose tipped back to follow the food, and before it was even dinnertime he was responding to just my voice without the food trick. My Dad left for a few hours in the afternoon to make a couple of deliveries and give someone a ride to the airport—he said he was using the truck to start his own little business, sort of a combination local FedEx and cab service—then he came home and made the broccoli soup I love. We ordered a pizza and had that for the main course, then we watched Terminator 2 and the first Star Wars prequel DVDs on the huge screen TV that takes up one whole wall of his living room. And then it was bedtime again. Since I drank a whole liter of Mountain Dew I could've probably watched six more movies without falling asleep, but my Dad was drinking beer the whole time and pretty much passed out on the couch. For a guy who works out all the time my Dad keeps a pretty good beer gut going.

It was weird. I mean we had a nice time together and everything. But I kept expecting him to ask me what was going on, why I wanted to stay with him. He knew about you, of course, but that was almost eight months before. I was just waiting for him to ask me what Mom and I were fighting about or to make some comment about David and how he figured I'd want to come live with him eventually, but he never said a word. It was like we'd had this visit planned for months or something. No, not even that really. It was more like I'd always lived with him and this was just another day in our lives together. Then the next day he made me go to church with him.

My Dad's family is Catholic and I used to go to church with

him a lot back when I was sleeping over on Saturday nights. We'd sleep in and go to the late service with all the old people who have nothing better to do with their Sundays. Mom grew up in the old Methodist church in Duquesne but joined David's Episcopal church even before they got married and that's where you and Em were baptized. My Dad calls Episcopals "JV Catholics" because they do almost everything like the Catholics except all the hard stuff, like they don't pay much attention to giving up stuff for Lent and their priests can get married, which even my Dad admits is looking more and more like a good idea since a wife's got to be better than an altar boy in the Lord's eyes any day of the week.

To me it seems like the main difference between the Catholics and Episcopals is money. And maybe microphones. I've been in a bunch of Catholic churches since all of my Dad's relatives live somewhere around Pittsburgh and since it seems like when a kid gets confirmed or someone gets married they invite every living member of the family tree excluding pets. Every Catholic church I've ever been in is either huge, old and ratty, or new, small and cheesy. In the huge old ones the priest is usually some geezer who's like 104 and needs a microphone to be heard even by the people in the front row who all have hearing aids the size of onions. In the new cheesy ones the priest is always one of those young wimpy-voiced guys who plays the guitar and says "super" a lot. And even if he doesn't really need the mike, all the money that would have gone to buy a huge organ if there'd been enough of it went to buy a synthesizer with chrome legs and a really bad sound system that makes the soloist at the wedding singing Ave Maria sound like she's on a cell phone from Cleveland. So if he's not using the mike it's like he's saying the church wasted that money. And if there's one thing the Catholics don't have to waste it's money.

If you're an Episcopal it seems like you can get by with Christmas and Easter plus maybe one Sunday a month as long as you give money. Our church is really beautiful if you remember. All white on the inside with wine-colored carpet and this enormous pipe organ that could blow the doors off an SUV. We haven't been back without you, but before you died we all probably went together every other Sunday or so, which is really good for Episcopals. If you're a Catholic you could put your whole paycheck in the platter, bring clothes right off your kids' backs and canned goods from your pantry for the poor every month but if you miss going to Mass a single time the flames of hell start to come up out of the floor around the bed where you're trying to sleep in for once. All that strictness is what gets them in so much trouble, I think. It's why they have to invent all these ways you can cheat, like even if you give up chocolate for Lent you can stuff your face with three pounds of Reese's Cups on Sunday because it's some kind of "Free Space," and like how you can go to a Mass so short on Saturday nights you can practically walk in one door crossing yourself and walk out the other and hear the whole thing. I bet any money a lot of the priests you see on the news these days had themselves convinced that fooling around with an altar boy was a way to not break their promise not to have sex. Doesn't count. Altar boy = Free Space.

The thing I hate most about Catholic churches, though, is they're so depressing they make anything that's sad even sadder because you're feeling sorry for the church on top of what you're sad about. Five summer friends of mine from the Lake were in a car accident a couple months before you died, and one kid I didn't know as well as the others was killed. There was a memorial service for him and it was at the Catholic church in town at the Lake. It was one of the huge old ones with the cathedral ceiling with paint chipping all over the place and a row of pews for practically every member of the church, but all the stuff on the wall behind the altar was new and cheesy. There was this huge, hollow-looking papier-mâché Jesus on a cross like forty feet tall that was set on top of what I guess was supposed to be the sun because there was this burst of three-dimensional orange and yellow beams coming out from behind him that looked like they'd been sprinkled with glitter by Em's art class. Then on either side of Jesus, much smaller, was a papier-mâché Mary and Joseph, just sort of floating out from the wall thirty feet apart, still in separate beds after all these years. God, it was depressing. I was such a mess Mom had to practically carry me out of there.

We walked to my Dad's church. It's one of the oldest Catholic churches in Pittsburgh and I think that's the only thing keeping it around. There are a lot of African Americans in my Dad's neighborhood but none of them go to his church. I try not to stereotype people too much but I don't think the Catholic church is ever going to be too popular with Black America until they do something about the music. If the Catholics do have any good hymns, they still sound terrible on the synthesizer with no choir and the soloist crackling through the speakers. That's one of the reasons Mom was okay with joining David's church. She said the Episcopals might have stolen a lot of stuff from the Catholics but they were smart enough to leave the hymns alone and steal those from the Methodists. Anyway, if a church isn't drawing from the African American population in my Dad's neighborhood, that's strikes one and two. Strike three is that hardly anyone who does go there has any money.

I didn't have any church clothes with me but if there's one good thing about the Catholic church it's that they don't seem to care what you wear as long as you show up. My Dad wore jeans and a clean T-shirt, which is what he wears just about every day of his life, and I wore white capri pants and a light blue tank top and the chunky sandals that make me about a foot taller. Mom and David never would have let me wear that to church but my Dad didn't say anything and neither did my Gram when we saw her there. She had great-gramma Mo Mo on her arm and Mo Mo didn't look like she cared much for my outfit but she didn't think most of my clothes were even appropriate for the pool, so she doesn't really count. Fortunately, her English has gotten even worse since she turned eighty-five so she doesn't say all that much. One time we were all in the waiting room at the hospital while my Dad's sister was being induced with her third child and, after they put the IV in, Mo Mo kept telling the other family members who came in that Mary Grace was "being seduced with an RV." Gram gave me a big hug and didn't seem surprised to see me and I kissed Mo Mo on her powdered cheek and then we all went in and sat down together.

I don't think you ever met my Gram but you would've liked her. She's big and soft and always smells like lipstick and perfume. Her hugs kind of fold you up like my Dad's but where my Dad is all hard from lifting weights you just kind of disappear into Gram. She's got these breasts that you can't believe and in all her old pictures she's wearing those bras that makes it look like she's got two wet-floor cones on under her sweater. She's not pretty now and didn't used to be either but she must have made the guys crazy with that body. When I was little my cousin Keira and I used to play with her bras and we'd each put one of the cups on our head and tie it under our chin and say we were Siamese twin nuns.

I have to admit that even though I didn't really want to come I was feeling better than I'd felt in a long time sitting there between Dad and Gram. Their smells kind of mixed with the mustiness of the church and surrounded me like a protective shield or something. My Dad's church still has an organ so the music didn't sound too bad, and they don't bother with a soloist, so it's just the congregation and the organ, no microphones. Gram kept reaching over and squeezing my knee looking straight ahead. The priest gave a nice sermon about the importance of family, our own and God's family, our family in heaven, and even though I had just left part of mine behind I felt like he was talking right to me there between my Dad and Gram. I hadn't been to church since you died, Mom won't go, and it was really helping to think of you being somewhere safe and beautiful. I felt like I could talk to you when we prayed and that everyone around me could feel me doing that and feel you there too.

But then it was time for Communion and Dad and Gram got up to go forward. I was baptized at Mom's Methodist church right after she left my Dad so I wasn't allowed to take Communion, which seems like another one of those rules that exists for no good reason that gets the Catholics in trouble. The Episcopals were smart enough to get rid of that one. It's right in the service at our church: "Anyone baptized in the Christian faith is welcome to take Communion at this altar rail." Anyway, my Dad and Gram couldn't have realized it but when they left they took their smells with them and I started to feel really alone. Mo Mo was still there but it seemed like she was ten feet away and had come to church by herself. While Dad and Gram were in line an assistant came back and gave Communion to all the people who couldn't leave their seats. When he came to Mo Mo he didn't even look at me. It was like he could feel I didn't belong there and that there was no chance I was sitting there because I had a disease or was paralyzed from the waist down or something. He just gave Mo Mo her wafer, said all the magic words and moved on. When Dad and Gram came back they motioned for me to slide over so I ended up sitting between Mo Mo and Gram and their smells didn't mix well at all and I started feeling kind of sick. I also started wondering what I was doing there and thinking about Em, who I hadn't thought about at all for the past three days, at least not the way I should have been thinking about her. I remembered how when Dad picked me up I was worried about leaving Mom alone when I should have been worrying about Em. I was the only person she could talk to and I'd left without saying anything. I started to get really hot and then the priest asked everyone to rise and sing the hymn they'd sung together every day since September 11th and the organist started playing "Let There Be Peace on Earth." I had never heard Catholics sing so loud. The organist pulled out all the stops and the place felt like it was shaking. Even my Dad who can't sing at all looked like he was straining to be heard and they all drowned out everything I had been thinking and their voices felt like they were pushing you up and out of the church. Before I even knew it was going to come out of me I was screaming "No! No! No!" as loud as I could but no one except Dad and Gram could hear me and Dad didn't even try to grab my arm when I pushed past him and ran out of the church. Which was a good thing because I wasn't stopping for anything.

# Just Wait

I thought I had learned about death last summer when my friends were in that car accident on the back road at the Lake. The one who was killed went through the sunroof and died in his best friend's arms. Another was in a coma for months and still can't speak or feed himself. The three who survived have constant nightmares. None of them had been drinking. None of them were bad kids. They'd just driven into town to pick up a movie, something we did all the time that summer, and were on their way back, driving too fast, the music up too loud, and they lost track of where the road rises to meet the railroad crossing. The police report said that the car must have been doing close to eighty when it took the crossing like a ski jump. If I'd been at the Lake that week I probably would have been with them, squeezed into the middle of the backseat or on someone's lap. I knew them only as well as you could know anyone you see a few weeks a year but I acted like their tragedy was my own. I was on the Internet constantly, IMing with the three who were okay, checking Matthew's condition, the one in a coma, offering my grief to all of them as something they could count on, something that showed I understood and would help them through. Gradually, all three of them stopped responding to me. They were nice about it, said they were busy now that they were back in school, said they wanted to start to try to forget. After you died, I knew why they'd stopped talking to me. I knew nothing before that car hit you and you landed without a sound at my feet. Nothing. Just like all the people who try to tell me how to feel about you know nothing. Just like all of the people in my school who write poetry about 9/11 for English class as if the fear they are feeling is the same as real loss. And just like all the people who lost no one, the tourists, who go to New York and cry over the rubble. I want to tell them all to go home. I want to tell them to go home and hold their children or their lovers or their parents. I want to tell them that they are using that place as an excuse to be sad and afraid when there will be reason enough for that in their own lives if they just wait.

*Em*

My Dad followed me out of the church. He didn't run or anything, like it was an emergency. He just came out like he was ready to go home and then that's what we did. We were supposed to go to my Gram's for an early dinner but we stayed home and ordered a pizza instead. I went to bed early and Frank came up with me.

I kept waking up all night thinking about Emily, so when my Dad dropped me off at school for the first time the next day, I told him to pick me up over at the elementary school at three-thirty. The elementary school where I went and where Em goes now is only about a ten-minute walk from the high school. When I got there the buses weren't even lining up yet, so I went around back and laid down under a tree in the playground. It was a tree I had climbed about a million times when I went to school there but Em says they don't even let the kids climb it anymore. I swear sooner or later parents will have invented ways to protect kids from their entire lives and we'll all just sit around and watch DVDs of digital kids who look just like us doing what we would be doing if it weren't so *dangerous*.

Anyway, I don't know how long I was lying there but I must have fallen asleep because Em's voice jolted me a little bit.

"Hey," she said. She was standing over me but looking back toward the school. I shielded my eyes to look up at her and I felt like it had been weeks instead of days since I'd seen her.

"Hey Em. School out already?"

"No. I was working at the terrarium and I saw you out the window and told Miss Ellenbogen I had to go to the bathroom."

Miss Ellenbogen was Em's first grade teacher, who took sort of a special interest in her after you died. She was always calling Mom to tell her how Em was doing, stuff she was noticing about her, stuff I don't think Mom was really ready to process in any helpful way, but Em loved Miss Ellenbogen.

"Isn't that kind of risky?"

She shrugged, still looking at the school. "I wanted to see you."

"Come here."

Em sat down beside me. She picked up a leaf and started gently pulling the leafy parts away from the thicker arteries.

I didn't know what to say so I just said, "How are you?"

"Okay."

"Mom?"

"Okay."

We were both quiet for a little bit and she worked on her leaf. She was pretty quick with it, like she'd practiced a lot, and it made me sad to think of her doing that out here while all the other kids were running around. When she held it up to me it looked like a tree skeleton, a miniature version of what the big tree would look like in winter.

"Cool."

She nodded and picked up another one. "Hey, Tess?"

"Yeah?"

"Are you coming home today?"

"I don't think so."

"When are you?"

"I don't know."

"Oh." She looked back toward what must have been Miss Ellenbogen's room again. "So how come you came here?"

"I don't know. I missed you. And I wanted you to know that me leaving didn't have anything to do with you."

"I know."

"Really?"

"Yeah."

"Good. That's good." I put my hand out to touch her shoulder and it was like she'd been waiting for it, like I'd released a spring, and her arms went around my neck and her feet went around my waist and I could feel in the pressure of her full-body grip on me how alone I'd left her.

"Hey there. Hey there," was all I could think to say, real softly, even though she wasn't crying. "I'll come see you here every day until school's over, okay?"

She nodded into my shoulder.

"You want a ride home today?"

She pulled back and her eyes got big at me. "You learned to drive?"

That cracked me up because even though she was so smart

and seemed so old sometimes, she seriously thought I could have left for three days and come back with a driver's license. I laughed at her and pushed her onto her back in the grass and started tickling her.

"No, silly." When you really get her going she can still sound like a baby when she laughs, bringing it from way down in her belly. When I stopped we were nose to nose and she smelled like the Tinkerbell perfume from the makeup set I'd given her for Christmas. "You want to ride with me and my Dad? He's picking me up here right when you get out."

"I don't know. I guess." She didn't look too sure. Em had never really warmed up to my Dad like you did.

"We'll follow the bus the whole way. Mom'll never know."

"Okay."

Then she said she better be getting back and she stood up and I watched her walk all the way to the door, then watched the top of her blond head appear and disappear in the windows of the breezeway between the two sections of the building, and then I even saw her face appear at the window where the terrarium must have been. She never looked up at me, she just went right back to what she'd been doing, and I wondered how she'd gotten to be so much stronger than me.

❧

Em was the last kid in her first grade class to lose a tooth and the space was on the bottom where you couldn't see it unless she smiled really big, which she hardly ever does. But when she saw my Dad's truck and looked around to see who was watching and the little puckered section of lower gum appeared, I realized

I couldn't have picked a better place for my Dad to pick me up. My friends would have crucified me for getting in that thing but Em knew the kids in her class would be all over her to find out how she was getting a ride home in such a cool truck.

"Hey, Em." My Dad greeted her first.

"Can we give her a ride home, Dad?"

"Sure. You want a ride, Em?"

Em nodded.

"I don't know where she's gonna sit."

"She can sit on my lap. Don't tell Mom, okay Em?"

I climbed up into the captain's chair, pulled Em after me and fastened the seat belt across both of our laps. There was no shoulder belt. Em was usually the safety police in the car, making sure everyone was buckled before Mom or David took the car out of park, but she was enjoying her moment of fame too much to care. A bunch of kids were pointing at her, some even calling her name, but she just looked forward through the windshield like she was Gwyneth Paltrow ignoring her fans or something. Her little lips were pursed together and I could tell she was trying not to smile because her cheek quivered a little bit.

I told my Dad to wait until all the kids were loaded up and the buses started to roll, and then we followed the whole line of them to the exit and turned with the half that turned left. We wound through the hills and buses pealed off every couple of streets and pretty soon we were following the only one headed down the hill toward the river. Nobody really said anything. Em let me rub her bare knees and she let herself fall back into me every time my Dad shifted. The bus didn't stop at all until we were down on the level and the sidewalks started in our neighborhood. At one stop, a boy got off and looked back and gave Em a big wave. She lifted her hand but probably not high enough for him to see.

As we got closer to our corner I found myself staring at the back of the bus, not wanting to look anywhere else. When the bus stopped, I put my face in Em's neck and hugged her to me. Our house was back over my right shoulder and I felt like it was looking at me.

"See you tomorrow, Em."

"Okay."

"Don't worry, okay?"

"Okay."

I released the buckle and she slid off my lap to the floor.

My Dad said, "Watch the holes," and she went around them like puddles, down the steep steps and out of the line of sight I was keeping.

She said, "Thanks," so softly I wasn't sure I'd even heard it but somehow my Dad did.

"No problem, sweetie. See you tomorrow." Then I could feel him look at me.

"You sure you don't want to get out too?"

"Yeah."

"Okay."

He waited to make sure Em got in safely, then my Dad wrestled the truck into gear and we headed home.

# *Jimmy Freeze*

It's weird how I'm starting to feel like you're grown up. Not on the outside. I still picture you as little. But I feel like I can tell you anything and you'll understand, even though you never got old enough to know about some of this stuff. Like about Jimmy Freeze.

In our neighborhood you can sit outside on your porch at night or take a walk, even in the summer when everyone's windows are open, and not hear much of anything except some crickets and once in a while a car going by. But in my Dad's neighborhood little pieces of people's lives come at you through all the ratty old screens. Sometimes it's laughing but usually it's a television or a stereo turned up really loud or a lot of times it's yelling. Even though we live in a neighborhood with sidewalks, the houses are a lot farther apart than at my Dad's and people could probably be as loud as they wanted and you wouldn't hear them unless you happened to be walking by. It's weird how it seems like even though people in my Dad's neighborhood live close enough to touch each other through their windows they don't care who hears what they're saying or doing. It's like the whole street is a dysfunctional family and the houses aren't really houses but different rooms in one big long house. At first it's just noise, like the crickets at home only deeper. But after a while your ears get pretty good at sifting through all the racket and picking out something to listen to. Sitting out on my Dad's porch at night is kind of like having fifteen or twenty stations devoted to reality radio, except there are police sirens about every two minutes. Taking walks is like slow channel surfing. Once, my Dad and I were walking Keisha and Frank and we passed a house where this couple was screaming like they wanted to murder each other and I asked Dad if we should call the police or anything. Mom and David never fought until recently, and even when they do it's more by not talking so I might be a little naive about stuff like that, but I never heard anyone talk to each other like Dad and I were hearing except in the movies, like in a Mafia film or something where the Italian wife finds out the husband has been keeping an apartment for some girl about eighteen. But my Dad said not to worry. When we passed again half an hour later they sounded like they were making their own porn video. My Dad started walking real fast but you had to be about six not to know what was going on in there.

The other weird thing about my Dad's neighborhood is that you can almost never see any stars. It's closer to the city than our house, plus with all the crime in the area they've put up enough streetlights to light a parking lot at the mall. That was hard for me to get used to at first because I'm used to seeing stars all the time. Mom and David stenciled the whole sky on my bedroom ceiling when I was about seven with this kit David bought at Nature's Wonders. Before bed he'd make me lie down and close my eyes while he turned on all the lights in my room to charge up the glow-in-the-dark paint. We'd count to fifty together and then he'd turn them all off and come and lie next to me. When I opened my eyes it was like we were out camping somewhere. He taught me all the constellations and after a while I was able to find them outside too. And not just the ones everybody knows, but other ones like Leo and Gemini and Draco the Dragon. When I asked my Dad if he could ever see stars in his neighborhood, he said, "You mean like movie stars?" and he was serious, so I just said to forget it.

The quietest house on the street was probably my Dad's next-door neighbor the Freezes. One of the reasons it was so easy to sit on the porch and listen to other people around the neighborhood was that there wasn't any interference close by. The house on the one side of us was vacant and the Freezes were in the other. They were this older Hungarian couple and even though I never heard of the Hungarian name "Freeze" before, we learned in school last year how lots of families lost their real names at the Statue of Liberty so I guess Freeze is possible. They lived by themselves, or that's what I thought until one night after I'd been with my Dad for a couple of weeks we heard yelling coming from their house. I was so used to having to listen hard to hear what was going on around us it was weird to have their voices hit us in the side of the head like that. It was mostly Mr. Freeze and another male voice that Dad told me was their son Jimmy, which didn't make sense to me. I had never actually seen Mrs. Freeze but Mr. Freeze looked like he was about seventy and Jimmy sounded pretty young. Not as young as me maybe, but he didn't have any of that deep, echoey quality in his voice grown-ups get.

Anyway, Mrs. Freeze was mostly crying while Jimmy Freeze and his Dad went at it and pretty soon Jimmy came flying through the screen door and took all the steps down to the sidewalk at once and headed up the street toward the flaming smokestack. He was tall and thin with curly hair a girl would kill for and his bony elbows flapped like wings when he ran. His house got quiet again and he never came back, at least not while my Dad and I were sitting there.

I fell asleep pretty early that night. Dad and I had to leave the house by 6:45 for him to get me to school on time, which was no picnic for either of us since I get my quality of not being a morning person from him. At about two o'clock in the morning two things woke me up at the same time. One was Frank standing on my chest and breathing in my face and the other was the music coming from the house next door. Once my Dad started selling Frank's brothers and sisters Frank started sleeping with me like I might be able to protect him. My Dad said nobody wanted the runt but I think he was telling them Frank wasn't for sale. Anyway, Frank never got up in the night so I guess the music must have woken him before it woke me and he wanted some company dealing with it. I admit I care a lot about what other people think but one thing I will never like no matter how cool it is is rap. I don't get it and I never will and apparently Frank and I had similar tastes because he was looking about as confused as I'd ever seen him. He kept looking to his left and then back at me for an explanation of the evil spirit that had invaded our walls. I lifted him off my chest and put him under the covers with me and tried to wait it out. If my Dad ever woke up he'd be outside and banging on the Freeze's door in about eight seconds but my Dad had his usual six beers on the porch and he woke up in the middle of the night exactly never.

The music pounded on my wall for what felt like six hours but was probably twenty minutes before I remembered my window was open and I got up to close it. When I peeked behind the blind I could see Jimmy Freeze's window just to the right and a little below mine. His blind was pulled too but I could see a dancing blue glow coming out from behind it from a TV or something. The music was so loud I couldn't believe his parents weren't making him turn it off. And it was that awful stuff, the really heavy, driving cop-killer stuff no white kid should even be allowed by law to listen to. I mean, you like rap, okay fine, I can deal with that. But you can't tell me you can relate to some gangbanger if you're a white kid, even a white kid from my Dad's crappy neighborhood, so don't even try to convince me. What he was listening to pissed me off almost as much as the fact that he was blasting it into my room at two A.M. and I got almost mad enough to lean out the window and yell at him myself and I would have if I thought he even had a 1 percent chance of hearing me over the woofers that must've been the size of kettledrums. So I just reached up to close the window, knowing it was going to do exactly no good whatsoever, and that's when I saw the shade flutter and someone walk past and the music stopped. I waited for a minute, my hands were still up over my window, looking at Jimmy Freeze's shade, and when it fluttered again and the music started again I felt dizzy and I had to lean my head against the screen to keep my balance. Because you'll never believe what he was playing. It was so out of place my brain refused to recognize it at first, but Jimmy Freeze was playing James Taylor singing "Sweet Baby James." And he was blasting it just as loud as he'd been blasting DMX a couple of seconds earlier. You know how sometimes when you're dreaming you can actually figure out you're dreaming and sort of control the magic for a little while until you're brain finishes waking up? I started to think that's what was happening. Because David used to play James Taylor all the time before you died and for a second I thought maybe I was dreaming that he was in the house next door. And since I could control the dream I made it so he was eighteen years old listening to the record by himself without any thoughts of you or me at all, but just using it to fall asleep after a date with a new girl he'd liked for a long time but never asked out before. I always pretended I didn't like James Taylor but even I had to admit he had about the best voice to fall asleep to I'd ever heard, and David doesn't play him at all anymore so that made it feel even more like a dream. I closed my window and came out from behind the blind and hurried up and got back into bed like I'd been doing something I shouldn't. I grabbed Frank and pulled him in with me and we lay there listening together. When the song ended it got quiet for a minute and then it started again. I don't know when I fell asleep or how many more times it played but I assume he never switched back to the rap because Frank never woke up again. That's the first night I ever spent with Jimmy Freeze.

# My Dad

Being with my Dad every day those first two weeks was a real eye-opener for me, even though I didn't find everything out right away. I mean, I'm not stupid. I've known my Dad was a screwup for a while but I never really knew how he went about it.

He basically does nothing. Not nothing nothing, like sitting around and watching TV, but the kind of nothing that can fill up your whole day. He goes to the gym. He works on whatever vehicle he's got to keep it mobile. And he always has at least six unfinished projects going on in the house. It used to belong to my Pap, one of his slum rental properties when he and Gram were still married, but when they got divorced they sold all of them except the "best" one, which they gave to my Dad. He says since he doesn't pay any rent he wants to put all his extra money into "improvements" so he can sell it. Who would want to buy a nice house in his neighborhood I don't know. He says he wants to buy the empty lot next to my Gram

82

and build a house himself, but if the time it takes him to patch a three-by-three hole in the drywall of the living room is any indication, there's no rush on the housewarming invitations. He spends a lot of time with his family too. I have eleven cousins from his older brother Tony and his younger sisters Geena and Theresa and I think he goes to every baseball game, wrestling match or school play that one of them's in. He's always going over to Gram's to fix something in her house and when he goes he usually comes home with dinner for both of us. Then he goes out maybe every other evening to make a few deliveries in the truck but never for very long. Getting up early to take me to school was something new for him and you might think he'd find something productive to do with those extra morning hours, but when I asked him once what he did after he dropped me off, he said he crawled into the back of the truck and took a nap and then went to Starbucks. And even though I'd kill for a nap every morning, it was kind of weird to hear a grown-up admit to it without sounding like he felt even a little bit guilty about it.

We fell into a routine pretty quickly but somehow the newness of it helped me, sort of forced me to concentrate on my days in blocks of minutes or hours instead of just letting them pass. I got in the shower at 5:45, stayed there until the hot water ran out, did my makeup, dried my hair, let the dogs out, then woke my Dad at about 6:30. I don't know why I got ready faster at my Dad's but I did. We'd eat cereal together with SportsCenter on in the background without saying much of anything. When I think about it, there were a lot of mornings neither of us said a word until we were almost to my school, like even though our bodies were in motion we were both waiting until the last possible minute to admit that the day had actually started. If you were watching us for the first time you might think we were mad at each other but we weren't. Dad was usually the one to break the silence:

"You got everything you need?"

"Yeah."

"You do your homework?"

"Mm-hm."

"Got money for lunch?"

"No."

"Here."

"Thanks."

"Am I picking you up here or at Em's school?"

"Em's"

"Three-thirty then?"

"Yeah."

"Love you."

"Love you too. Bye."

"Bye."

The part about doing my homework was just conversation. He never asked me that question at night. It was weird, though. David rode me all the time about homework and I was always forgetting to do stuff, forgetting about tests. I didn't do it on purpose, I wasn't trying to rebel or anything, it just happened. With my Dad it was like I knew he'd never remember to ask so I started remembering on my own. I'm not saying I became a star or anything. My grades had already gone to shit and it was too late to do much about it but at least I didn't end up having to repeat tenth grade, which for a while was no guarantee let me tell you.

Anyway, he picked me up at the elementary school pretty much every day and he was usually on time, which I knew meant he was trying real hard. Sometimes Em rode the bus home but mostly she came with us. She never looked at my Dad if he was talking to her but she started answering his questions looking out the window and I could tell she was starting to like him. She never asked when I was coming home again until the last day of school, but I'll tell you about that later.

When Dad and I got home I'd do my homework. My Dad doesn't have a computer so I couldn't chat online with my friends and I had to do all my typing in the computer center at school but it wasn't too bad. Every couple of days before bed I'd call and talk to Mom for a little bit. Once she realized I was staying for a while she started to get real sad on the phone, apologizing all over the place and telling me the thing with Justin was nothing, just something stupid I'd understand some-day and not to worry about it. I told her I didn't leave because of that but I don't know if she believed me because she kept on saying she was sorry over and over again. I told her she was saying sorry to the wrong person and she got real quiet. Other than that we got along okay.

Most nights my Dad and I just hung out at home, out on the porch or walking the dogs or watching sports or a movie. My Dad never went out at night although I got the feeling that wasn't always the case because people called all the time and he just told them, No, not tonight, like it was an excep-tion. Sometimes people came to the door, but if it wasn't fam-ily he'd talk to them real low at the door and come back and say it was no one. When I was little and used to sleep over at my Dad's a lot he always had a girlfriend. It was never the same one for very long and most of them were these total bimbos from the gym who were always trying to bribe me to go to bed early, which they were too stupid to figure out just made me want to stay up later. But there weren't any girls those first couple of weeks either. It was almost like Dad and I were on vacation together again, somewhere we didn't know anybody. Although my Dad's street wasn't exactly Disney World.

Something else you should know about my Dad is he still keeps the wedding picture of him and Mom on his dresser. You wouldn't even recognize her. I mean, it's Mom and she's still pretty and everything, but not beautiful like now. And she's so young. Not just young to be getting married, but not much different than some of my friends. It looks like a prom picture more than a wedding picture. My Dad has on this really bad white tux with a ruffled shirt that has a little blue just on the ends of the ruffles and he has all this really curly black hair that must have all fallen out before my first memory of him. Mom's dress is real simple, just like you'd expect, except she's so skinny it kind of pooches away from her bony shoulders and it seems like you could look right down at her boobs if you were up above her. Her hair is all Farrah Fawcetty and her head is on my Dad's shoulder real corny, like you see in the newspaper announcements, and her smile is kind of nervous, especially in her eyes. It looks like she knows she's making a mistake but she's just trying to get through the day so she can start figuring out what to do next. Or maybe that's my imagination since I already know the rest of the story, but I can't figure out why my Dad would want to look at that picture every day, even if he still loves my Mom, which is something

I'm not really sure about. The only thing I can think of is it's a picture of one of the only really important days of his life and he needs to be reminded that he once did something that was worth doing, even if it didn't work out so great. I don't know.

# Soul Man

Jimmy Freeze came and went from his house at least five times a day. I spent a lot of time on my Dad's porch and I bet there was hardly a single time I sat out there more than an hour that Jimmy Freeze didn't either come running out of his house or jogging up the sidewalk and take his steps two at a time. I figured he was seventeen, maybe eighteen, but it was hard to tell because he was so tall. He was always in a hurry but he was never carrying anything, at least nothing that didn't fit in his jeans pockets.

He also never acknowledged my existence and that started to make me think he was cuter than maybe he was, which I *hate*. Getting older makes you stupid that way. I mean, he was cute but there was nothing all that unique or mysterious about him, except that he paid absolutely *no* attention to a girl who wasn't that much younger than him, no matter what she wore. I started to get a feel for his schedule and made sure I was sitting out there whenever he might come by but I may as well have been a pot of flowers. So I figured I needed to make an impression.

It had been a while since the night his music woke me up and it had never happened again. Frank and I were sitting on the porch steps, directly in his line of sight as he fast-walked up the sidewalk. He somehow turned and started up his stairs without ever registering our presence, until I started singing.

I sang real soft, "There is a young cowboy . . . who lives on the range . . ."

You never saw anybody stop so fast in your whole life. He was like David Blaine with his hand on the handrail and his legs levitating in mid-air. Then he rocked back off the steps.

"What did you say?"

He looked a little bit like he was in one of those dreams where you realize you've gone to school in your underwear.

"Me?"

"No. The dog."

"Nothing."

"What song was that?"

"I don't even know. Just some stupid thing my stepfather used to play. It's been stuck in my head lately for some reason. Frank likes it." I stroked Frank's head and he played along real well. His tongue was hanging out sideways.

"That your dog?"

"Not really. My Dad's selling a litter and no one wants this one so far."

"How come?"

"I don't know. He's the runt, I guess."

"You gonna keep him if no one takes him?"

"You always ask so many questions before you find out someone's name?"

"Sorry." He actually did look sorry. "What's your name?"

"I'm Tess."

"Hey Tess, Jimmy." He let go of the rail and put out his hand. He had long fingers and his hand was real warm.

I nodded at his house. "You live there?"

"Yeah, sometimes. With my Dad and my stepmom."

"I'm surprised I haven't seen you before."

"I'm out a lot."

"Yeah? Where?"

"Nowhere really. Just around. Pretty much anywhere but here. He friendly?" Jimmy put his hand out to Frank and Frank sat up and put both paws on either side of it, like he was holding a lollipop, and licked it real fast.

"Yeah, he's friendly. How about you?"

It was like he sort of looked at me for the first time. "Depends."

"On what?"

He sat down on the steps so Frank was between us and he started scratching his ears. Frank's whole head fit in his hand.

"You Nunz's daughter?"

"You know my Dad?"

"Sort of."

"Sort of how?"

"Sort of how everyone knows him."

"How's that?"

"I don't know. He's just one of those guys people sort of know. Plus the truck. I mean, you can't have a truck like that and not have people say, 'Who the fuck was that?'"

"What's that supposed to mean?" I couldn't believe I was defending the truck. "You got a Porsche or something?"

"I'm not exactly legal to drive right now."

"How come?"

"Let's just say if I'd had a license during my last traffic stop it would have been suspended again."

"You think that's pretty cool?"

"No. I think it sucks."

"Because I'd kill for a driver's license right about now. And when I get it I don't think I'm going to treat it like a bad girlfriend."

"How old are you?"

"Sixteen. Soon."

He looked at me like he was surprised but couldn't decide why.

I said, "You're thinking my face looks older but my body looks younger."

"Yeah. That's it. How'd you know?"

"How'd I know what I look like?"

"Hey, no worries. Sorry."

"Look. I was practically the first girl in my class to get my period and I'm either the last one to get boobs or this is it." I looked down at myself.

He turned sort of red and looked at Frank. "Either way. No worries."

"For you."

"Yeah, for me." He kept looking at Frank. "Not a boob man." He said it real soft, like boys talk to Mom.

"No such thing."

"I'm telling you."

"Then what are you?"

"I'm an eyes man." He still wasn't looking at me.

"An eyes man. Yeah."

"A 'Soul Man.'" He did a little Belushi thing with his voice, that dead guy from *SNL*.

He grabbed Frank's paws and stood him up on his back legs and sort of hid behind him while he sang.

"'Cause you ain't seen, nothin' yet. I'm a Soul Man! I'm a Soul Man!"

It was pretty funny but I pretended I didn't think so.

"Very mature."

He looked at me from behind Frank. He squinted a little bit.

"How come you wear so much makeup?"

"You're real smooth, you know that?"

"No, I mean you don't need it. That's all."

"Thanks."

"So why do you?"

"I don't know. I think I like putting it on more than I like how it looks when I get it on. I feel like I'm making a different person."

"Why would you want to do that?"

"Why wouldn't you?"

He shrugged at me. "Hey, you got anything to drink inside?"

"Sure. You want a beer or something?" I don't know why I asked him that.

"Your dad won't mind?"

"Naw. He gives me sips of his all the time. Hold on to Frank."

I went inside and walked through the living room, where my Dad was on the couch watching the Pirates and into the kitchen. I took a beer out of the refrigerator and headed back through the living room, trying to look like I did this every day. My Dad did sort of a double take.

"Where you goin' with that?"

"Porch."

"Who's out there with you?"

"That kid from next door. Jimmy, I think. He's real nice and I told him you wouldn't . . ."

"Put it back."

"Dad!"

"Put it back and come inside. You're not hangin' around with him."

"Why not?"

"Because I said so."

"What am I supposed to do, Dad? Hang out with you all summer?"

"You can have friends from school over here."

"Dad, come on."

He didn't act like a dad or lose his temper with me very often, so it kind of scared me when he got up off the couch and stood real close to me.

"Either you go out and tell him to leave, or I will. And you ain't gonna like how I do it."

"Okay, okay."

I set the beer down and went out to the porch. Jimmy had put Frank down and was already standing up.

"No worries. I heard him."

"Sorry. I don't know what his problem is."

"Me. It's going around." He hopped over the handrail and down to the little strip of concrete between our houses. He pointed up and into the narrow alley. "Your room that one?"

"Yeah."

He nodded backward, down to up. "See you, Tess DeNunzio."

"Bye."

Frank and I went inside. I picked up the beer, twisted off the lid and took a sip. My Dad didn't say anything.

# Travis

Jimmy was right about my Dad's truck. It became a part of his identity. People neither of us even knew started waving to us on the way home from school. Really it was more like they were greeting the truck since they never looked to see if we waved back. The truck was like this mobile member of the community everybody recognized. Even Frank. I know dogs are supposed to know things mostly by smell, but he'd see Dad's truck turn the corner into our block and he'd go leaping off the porch to greet him.

"See, Tess," he told me once, before I knew the real reason why a lot of them were waving. "This truck's got character. No one's got character no more."

I told him *having* character wasn't the same as *being* a character, which is what he was in that thing.

"Nothin' wrong with that either," he told me.

And I guessed he was right, though I was still glad he mostly picked me up over at Em's school.

Maybe you put the clues together already but it took me longer than you might think to figure out he was dealing drugs from the back of that thing. I don't know how I thought he was making money enough to live, let alone work on the house and buy a TV the size of a billboard. There couldn't have been that many "deliveries" in his neighborhood worth paying someone for except the obvious, and people with enough money to be flying somewhere weren't likely to want to arrive at the airport jumping out of the back of the S.S. 'Nunz like some underprivileged SWAT team.

I found out from this really creepy guy who came right up on the porch one day after school. Frank and I were just relaxing and this guy comes up and drops a roll of twenties at Frank's front feet like a bone. Frank sniffed it and the guy looked at me for like ten minutes before he said anything.

"You Nick's girl?"

I didn't like the way he said that so I said no, I was his daughter. He smiled out of one side of his mouth like he thought he was a villain in a movie. He was real skinny and even though he looked about forty he had pimples all over the loose skin on his long neck and he had eyes like an old dog, all yellow and weepy.

He said, "That so? You remember me?"

"Nope."

"I'm Travis. Me and your Dad went to high school together. I was at your folks' wedding."

"Sorry. Wasn't there."

He didn't laugh but his eyes got shinier.

"No. But I seen you lots before your Mom got smart and

left. Probably even seen you naked a couple times." My skin got all jumpy when he said that and I looked down at Frank so he wouldn't see I was afraid. "Can't believe enough time's passed for you to look like this." I saw the toe of his dirty sneaker nudge the roll of twenties away from Frank who was licking it.

"You mind giving that to your Dad for me?"

"Why?"

"Your Dad takes care of his old friends and this is an old debt."

"Sure. Whatever."

"Thanks, honey pie." He bent over to give Frank's head a quick pat but I could feel him still looking at me. "You ever get to sample the product?"

"Excuse me?"

"Come on. The way kids are now and you livin' at the warehouse? You gotta be an old pro."

"I don't know what you're talking about." Although by then I had a pretty good idea.

"Whatever you say. Your Dad gone for a while?" Now I looked up because I wanted to be ready just in case. Travis pulled a half-smoked joint out of his shirt pocket. "I still got a little left."

"He's on his way home. Right now." And as if I'd made it appear, the truck came around the corner and headed straight for us. Frank leapt off the porch, kicking the twenties down the steps. I felt like following him but I didn't want to give Travis the satisfaction.

Travis said, "Too bad. Maybe another time," and then he wasn't far behind Frank. He tried to seem casual about it but he didn't look like he had much interest in paying my Dad in person. He waved at the truck without looking up and headed down the sidewalk.

As of that moment I'd never smoked weed in my life but I wasn't naive about it. Most of my friends had at least tried it and a few kids I'd hung out with in middle school left it behind for bigger stuff a long time ago. I don't think there are less drugs in good schools like mine, just more expensive ones. Still, watching my Dad get out of his truck, see him see Travis, see him see the roll of twenties at the foot of the stairs, see him figure out what I probably knew made me feel older all of a sudden, like when I found out about Mom and Justin. My Dad had his head down a little and I was sitting way above him like a judge. He bent to pick up the money, flipped it in the air and grabbed it again and Frank jumped, thinking it was a game. He ignored Frank and looked up, right at me, to see what I was going to do.

"Aren't you scared?" I asked him.

"Of what?"

"Of getting caught."

"I guess I'm more scared of not havin' any money."

"How about work, Dad?"

"It ain't that easy."

"Yes it is, Dad. You work, they pay. That easy."

"Not what I'm worth. You know, I want to be able to give you stuff."

"How does anyone know what you're worth, Dad? You never stay long enough for them to figure it out." He was sitting next to me now. Frank looked up at us from the walkway, back and forth. "And don't hand me any more crap about doing it for me.

You've got satellite and a DVD. How much money's in my college account?"

"Okay. News flash: I'm a shitty father."

"No you're not. But from prison, yes. From prison you'd be a really shitty father."

"It's nothin'. A little weed. Only to adults. And never enough to sell to anyone else."

"Oh great. My Dad, the dealer with a conscience."

"They're gonna get it from someone."

"So it may as well be you?"

"Exactly."

"Jesus, Dad. Are you familiar with 'The War on Drugs'? Do you ever watch the news on that theater in your living room?"

"Sweetie, in 'The War on Drugs,' I'm a conscientious objector."

People like my Dad a lot. Even David and people who think he's wasted his life, because he either makes you think he's doing exactly what he wants to be doing and wouldn't trade places with you in a million years, or he makes you laugh.

"The warden will love your sense of humor, Dad."

"I'm serious. That's my political position."

"You don't even vote."

"If I did."

"So people should be able to buy drugs like groceries."

"I'd put little bells on the truck. Like the Goody-Bar man."

"Brilliant."

"You know. All the burnouts would hear the bells and come racin' out. But real s-l-o-w." He dragged out that last word and made his voice drop down low. He was nudging me with his shoulder to ask if we were done arguing and I nudged him back, but real hard, to say yes but not because he'd won. Frank sensed the end of the conflict and scrambled up the stairs to push his head between us and we all went inside to figure out what to do for dinner. That was the way fights with my Dad always ended, at least for me—with food. Apparently it wasn't that way for everyone though. I passed Travis on the sidewalk a few days later, and even though he tried to look away I could see he had a shiner on his left eye about the size of a hockey puck. He was lucky I hadn't told my Dad everything he said.

# Stoned

I don't want this to come out the wrong way but it was easier to forget about you at my Dad's, especially once Jimmy Freeze and I started hanging out together. When I was at home everything old was still there except you so I could never look anywhere or even *be* anywhere without feeling like you should be there too. Jimmy was something new in a new place and it helped take up the space where you were. I even started to understand about Mom and Justin and I felt bad for her that the one thing that maybe made her feel better for a little while was something just about the whole world would see as wrong.

Jimmy Freeze disappeared for a few days after Dad made me kick him off the porch. Or at least if he was around he didn't show himself to me, and I looked for him plenty. I don't think I'm one of those girls who's attracted to "bad boys." Most of the boys like that at my school are sort of poseurs who aren't bad because they're really bad but because they can't figure out how to be what they actually are. I think what I liked about

Jimmy Freeze was that he felt like the opposite of that—like he was really a good guy who couldn't help himself from screwing up a lot. Sort of like my Dad, not to get all Freudian or anything.

Anyway, the night I found out about his little "business" with the truck, my Dad and I made a huge dinner and sat in front of the TV eating until almost nine o'clock. Then I did homework while he drank beer and fell asleep in front of the Pirates, who were on the West Coast. I don't know if it was a coincidence or not but no one called, no one came to the front door, nothing. By the time Frank and I threw a blanket over him and headed upstairs, it was close to midnight.

I heard the music as soon as I went in my room, not because it was as loud as last time, but because I guess I'd been listening hard for sounds from his house for days. It was the same song again, soft and low, but my window was open and I guessed his was too.

> Goodnight you moonlight ladies,
> Rockabye sweet baby James.
> Deep greens and blues are the colors I choose.
> Won't you let me go down in my dreams,
> And rockabye sweet baby James.

God, what sappy stuff. But for some reason it made me feel really good to think about lying in bed and listening to it with him. Not *with* him, I guess, but that's what it felt like. I switched off the light and Frank and I settled in. I think I would have been asleep in about five minutes if I hadn't heard what sounded like a scratching at the screen. I wasn't sure I'd heard anything until I looked at Frank and saw that his little ears were two perfect triangles pointing straight up, along with the hair at the base of his neck. I told him "Shhh," and we listened together. It came again, louder this time. We both jumped out of bed and ran to the window and when I pulled back the shade I could see what looked like the white blade of a street-hockey stick against the screen. My heart just about ricocheted off the walls of my chest because I've seen all those *Halloween* movies and my imagination put Jason and his white hockey mask at the other end of that stick. Who it was of course was Jimmy Freeze leaning out his window below me.

"Hey, Tess DeNunzio," he said.

I automatically put my finger to my lips but I don't know why. His parents let him play music that shook the house and my Dad was downstairs in a Coors Light coma.

"Wanna come over?" he whispered. He was motioning for me to come out my window.

God, I wanted to more than anything.

"I can't," I whispered back.

"Why not?"

I gestured to my windowsill and then to his like a game show hostess, telling him there was no way I could make it. His window wasn't that far below mine but it was far enough to the right to make it too big a stretch for me.

"Then I'll come up," he said. He crawled out and stood on the sill. From there he could lean out and prop himself against my Dad's house. He stretched over, grabbed my sill, and before I could tell him not to he had let his feet fall away from his house and was hanging below me.

"Hey, Tess," he said.

"Yeah?"

"How about opening the screen?"

"Oh yeah. Right."

All the windows in my Dad's house were new and the screen slid up easily and Jimmy Freeze scrambled up and in.

"Nice work, Spidey." I tried to sound like boys scaled buildings to see me all the time.

"Thanks."

Frank was over the initial shock of a body coming through the window and was working himself up to bark until Jimmy put his hand out. Quick as that, Frank settled and started licking Jimmy's hand like a salt stick. We both watched him and Frank's tongue was all you could hear for maybe a whole minute.

"Okay," I said. "Now what?"

Jimmy looked at me and smiled a little bit, but let Frank keep licking his hand.

"You ever get high?"

"Not really."

"Not really?"

"No."

"Wanna try?"

"Sure."

"I mean, it's just weed. No big deal. We could sit on the windowsill."

"I said *okay*."

"Oh."

It was as simple as that, really. I think parents have this

view that their kids are being pressured all the time to do drugs and maybe some kids are, but I guess I was just waiting for someone to ask. Someone other than Travis. Or at least someone like Jimmy Freeze. I mean if my own Dad was selling the stuff how bad could it be?

We sat facing each other on the windowsill and listened to the music rising up from his room. He had really nice eyes, dark and set deep, and I could tell he was taking this seriously, that he wouldn't make fun of me if I coughed up half a lung or something. He reached into his jeans pocket and pulled out a lighter and a little cigarette case that had four freshly rolled joints in it. He took one out, lit it, took a longer drag than I'd ever seen any of my friends take and held the smoke for what seemed like a minute.

"This how you know my Dad?" I asked.

He turned and exhaled, filling the space between our houses with swirling smoke. "Yep. This and being neighbors."

"Is that why he made me kick you off the porch?"

"I don't know. I guess. Or maybe he knows some of the other stuff. Here." Jimmy handed me the joint. "For the first couple, don't even put your lips around it. Just bring it real close and whistle in."

"Like this?"

"Yeah. You won't get as much smoke and it'll be cooler."

"Okay."

I coughed a little but it wasn't as bad as I thought. We passed it back and forth a few times, Jimmy taking huge drags, me barely making the tip turn red. Frank watched us from the bed.

"What other stuff?" I asked him.

"About the school I go to and why I'm there and everything. My Dad sent me there but he holds it against me."

"What kind of school?"

"One of those places for 'troubled youths.' Way up in Maine. Costs my Dad more money than he's got and it's mostly rich kids who never had any idea how lucky they were. Anyway, my Dad's not stupid. He knows I still smoke pot. But I was doing a lot of other stuff before. He can't understand that smoking pot and doing nothing else practically makes me a geek up there. He thinks just because it's basically a correctional facility everyone who goes there gets 'corrected.' Most of the kids are just happy to be away from their parents so they can do their drugs in peace."

I told him about Kasey, about her getting arrested on our porch and being sent to a school like that and then getting kicked out.

"Yeah. Half of my class has been kicked out. You feelin' anything?"

"I'm not sure."

He smiled. "You'll be sure. Put your lips around it this time and take in a little more. It's gonna be hotter."

I could feel the smoke singe the back of my throat on the way in but I held it.

"You're a natural."

I shrugged, still holding it in. That's when I started to feel every pore in my body open up at once. Jimmy must have seen it happening.

"There you go," he said. "No worries."

From there the whole night slowed down. And for a while got real funny. Nothing that had ever happened to me in my life was as funny as Jimmy Freeze putting his face real close to mine to check out my pupils. Until he lost his balance and almost fell out the window into the alley and that turned out to be even funnier. Then after a while I was able to relax into the high and Jimmy Freeze and I started solving all of the world's problems: poverty, hunger, killing in the name of religion. It all seemed so simple. Just a matter of a little human kindness and understanding. Nothing JT and us couldn't handle. Like Jimmy said, No worries. Then he started talking about New York, the Towers. I nodded, got quiet, didn't tell him about you. He told me about his real Mom and how she died when he was ten and he showed me the picture of her he carries everywhere. In the picture she's dark and beautiful. She's starting to look away and two surprisingly thin fingers are covering one side of her face, like someone had snuck up on her with the camera and she was embarrassed. Jimmy said she hated having her picture taken that last six months. He asked if my Mom was still around, did I have brothers or sisters, did I have pictures. I told him about Mom and Em and David, said I hadn't brought any pictures with me.

"You okay, Tess?"

I said I was just real tired all of a sudden.

"You'll sleep like a baby. And no hangover. That's the beauty."

"Great."

"Hey." I must have been looking down because all of a sudden his finger was under my chin, pulling my eyes up to his face. "Thanks for letting me be your first. You sure you're okay?"

"Perfect."

"Wanna do this again sometime?"

"Yeah. I do."

"Can I kiss you good night?"

"Yeah. You can."

And he kissed me just like I hoped. Real soft. Just lips. And real long. At least I think it was real long. It was still hard to tell. Then he swung his legs out the window, braced his hands on the sill, his feet flat against his own house, and shimmied his way down until he could reach his right foot over and step down. After he'd slipped inside he poked his head back out and put up a finger for me to wait. Then he disappeared for a minute and came back with a spray can. He mimed a throw then threw for real, and somehow I caught it. Lysol.

"Keep it," he said. "For next time."

"Thanks."

"Night, Tess DeNunzio."

"Night."

I slid the screen down, pulled the blind and sat down heavy next to Frank. He looked up at me like he was jealous. Or suspicious. Like he knew I was stoned. Or maybe he just looked like that *because* I was stoned. Because all of a sudden, alone, without another stoned human being in the room to balance me out, I was the most stoned human being that had ever lived. And the hungriest.

I made my way down the stairs and into the kitchen in a time warp. Inside the frig was pizza from God knows when but I started eating, standing right there with the refrigerator door wide open because the thought of taking the time to close it was too much. Frank sat in the triangle of light at my feet, his tail twitching, his eyes following every bite of pizza to my mouth until I started sharing.

"Don't tell Dad," I whispered. "Don't tell him anything."

# Leaving Em Again

On the last day of school kids ran out of the front of Em's building like it was burning. Backpacks were half on one shoulder or
dragging on the ground and papers they'd been saving all year
were falling out of notebooks and being left behind. They
shouted and turned and waved to their teachers and then their
buses sucked them in like high-speed vacuums. I wished I could
still feel that way about the end of school, forgetting as soon as
I got off the bus at home that there was even such a thing as
next year. But now every year feels less and less like an ending
and closer and closer to the beginning of something I'm not
ready for. That's how Em looked, like she was seventeen instead of seven. She walked real slow and didn't look up even
though she knew I was there.

"Hey Em, happy summer," I said.

"Mm." She nodded and walked past me toward where my
Dad's truck was parked. I followed and climbed in behind her,

pulled her into my lap and buckled us in. I guess my Dad could see there was something going on so he stayed quiet.

We pulled out and followed the buses to the exit. Through the back windows of the one in front of us we could see kids bouncing up and down in their seats and balls of paper flying across the aisle. A boy pressed his face and hands to the window, crossed his eyes and pushed his tongue between his flattened lips.

I said, "That a friend of yours, Em?"

She shook her head.

"Aren't you glad you don't have to ride the bus with those morons?"

She shrugged.

"You okay?"

Another shrug.

"I mean if you're going to give me the silent treatment I think I at least have a right to know why, don't you?"

"I guess."

"Well?"

We drove for a while without saying anything. I could tell she wasn't just trying to annoy me so I didn't push her. After a while she sat back against me and I felt her relax.

"So when am I going to see you now?" she said.

"What do you mean?" I knew what she meant but I was stalling for time to think up an answer.

"I see you at school every day. School's over now, so when am I going to see you?"

I still didn't know what to say and it made me feel like a parent. Whenever they have to think about their answers and they give you one of those long, well-reasoned explanations, you know they're lying. I decided not to do that to Em.

"I'm not sure," I told her.

"Why not?"

"I need some time to think about some things."

"Like what?"

"Lots of things, I guess. Will you be okay on your own for a while?"

"I've *been* on my own."

"I know. I mean even a little bit more."

She moved her small shoulders. It wasn't much more than a twitch. "I don't know. I guess."

She was quiet but pretty soon it seemed like she was breathing a little faster and I could tell she was trying not to cry.

"It's not fair," she said.

"What?"

"I have to miss both of you at the same time. It's not *fair*."

"Em?"

"You and Zoe. No one thinks I miss her."

She started to cry.

"Of course we do."

"*No!*" She yelled really loud, which she never does, so it scared me. "Then why don't I get to do anything about it? Mom gets to lay on the couch and sleep all the time. Daddy gets to stay at work all night. You get to leave like you're not even in our family anymore. What am I supposed to do?" She was crying hard now. "I do everything just like before, Tess! I do everything the same! I'm the littlest one left and no one's telling me what to do!"

I held her real tight. "Shh. Hey."

"It's not fair!"

"No."

"I can't stop missing her."

"No. No one can. No one should."

"But how much longer?"

"I don't know. Maybe forever."

"Don't say that, Tess. Don't say that."

"Do you really want to stop missing her?"

"No. I just want it to stop hurting so much."

"It will."

"When?"

"I don't know."

"Has it for you?"

"No."

Then as fast as it had come on, she got quiet again and curled in my lap under the seat belt. My Dad reached a hand across and put it on her leg and she let him keep it there. We rode like that the rest of the way.

When we turned onto our block I could see someone standing at the corner stop by our house watching kids get off the bus. By the time it pulled away I could see that it was David. He was still in his suit from work and he was looking after the bus with his hands in his pockets, seeming a little confused. I don't think he'd ever seen this particular truck of my Dad's either, so turning and seeing us coming didn't help any until he saw my Dad waving at him.

My Dad patted Em's leg. "Hey Em, look who's here."

Em looked up. "Daddy!"

When David waved back, I couldn't help it. I turned away.

"Keep going, Dad."

"What?"

"Keep going. I don't want to see him right now."

"Tess, honey, I can't just go driving by with his daughter."

"Just go, Daddy! Please!"

"Stop! Stop!" Em shouted.

"Tess, I can't." My Dad pulled over and opened the door and Em wiggled out of the belt, jumped down the stairs and up into David's arms.

"You're home! How come you're home?"

"Hey, sweetie. Happy summer." He turned his body left and right as he hugged her, like rocking a baby. Over Em's shoulder he said, "Nick," and my Dad nodded.

Then David said, "Hey, Tess."

"Hey."

I was studying one of the holes in the floor of the truck. The rust around the edges looked like dried blood, a scab.

"You doing okay?"

"Fine."

Out of the corner of my eye I could see Em's feet appear next to David's on the sidewalk. One of her hands was at her side so the other must have been in his.

"Is there anything you need? I mean, anything I can get from your room for you to take with you?"

"No."

"Okay. If you're sure."

"I'm sure."

"Everything's okay then?"

I nodded.

"We miss you, you know. Your Mom and Em, all of us."

"Okay."

No one said anything for a while. I started poking at the edges of the scab with my shoe and brick-colored dust floated to the pavement under the truck.

Then David said, "Okay then," and cleared his throat. "Hey, Tess?" I started to look up. I swear I *wanted* to look up at him, I even wanted to tell him I missed him too but I couldn't. "Maybe you could call your mother a little more often, like you did at first. I think she's been missing that."

I didn't say anything right away, so my Dad said, "I'll make sure she calls."

"Thanks, Nick."

"No problem."

"Really. Thanks for everything. You'd let us know if you needed anything, right?"

"We're doin' fine, but yeah."

"Okay then."

Without realizing it I must have been pushing harder and harder against the rusted edges of the hole with the toe of my shoe because right then my whole sneaker pushed through the floor of the truck and I probably would have fallen out of my captain's chair up to my hip if I wasn't still belted in.

My Dad said, "Don't move!" and jumped up to help me pull it out slowly without scraping my bare shin on any of the sharp edges. He had to straddle the weak parts of the floor and I could tell he was embarrassed because he kept talking while he was helping me, partly to himself but mostly to David, about how he was just about to weld an extra piece of sheet metal to the underside of the frame and how he guessed he'd waited one day too long and how he'd been thinking about trading this big old pile of junk in on one of those little foreign cars, a Honda or a Toyota, something that wasn't breaking down every other week and how if he weren't putting so much money into the house so he could sell it he'd probably have that new car already. David must have known that it just would have made it worse if he stepped up into the truck to help, so he and Em just stood on the sidewalk and were quiet.

When my foot was free I was looking through a hole the size and shape of a football. The flakes of rust, some big some small, lay on the road not far from where you stepped off the curb that day, and they were arranged in a pattern that was like some form of hieroglyphics I was supposed to understand. I only partly heard my Dad and David saying their good-byes as I studied it, trying to figure out what it was saying to me. My vision blurred then got sharp again and the pieces seemed to rearrange themselves into a message I could recognize with enough time, but then the truck was moving and the words slipped under me like credits going in reverse. I looked up into the big square side mirror just in time to see David leading Em through our yard and Em resisting his pull to watch us disappear.

# Dolls

Em was right of course. It was easy to forget how much she must have missed you.

I remember when you were just old enough to start playing with dolls, really pretending, and Em couldn't get enough of playing with you. She was real patient, showing you how to hold a baby, put it in the high chair, always going along when you wanted to do the same things over and over again. But what she really loved was when you got the hang of pretending to be a baby yourself. That amazed her, that a little person who wasn't much more than a baby could pretend to be one, almost like you first had to pretend to be older just to have that ability. She'd rock you in the little rocker in her room, read you stories from memory, hold a bottle to your lips while you made kissing noises. Then she'd set you in the bottom half of a plastic under-bed storage bin that was supposed to be your crib, pull her blinds, turn on her nightlight and leave the room. "Call Mommy when you wake up," she'd say, "or if you have a bad dream." Sometimes if I was doing homework or listening to music or something she'd come in my room while she waited for you to call. You got to be so good at it sometimes she had to peek in to check and make sure you hadn't really fallen asleep. That was so unlike you, staying quiet for so long. It was like you were trying to prove yourself to Em. Then finally you'd call and Em would look at me and roll her eyes as if to say a mother's job was never done. And then she'd open the door on you, and you'd still be lying in the bin, smiling, reaching for her.

# Skycooster

Em had nothing to help her forget you, even for a little while. I had Jimmy Freeze climbing in and out of my life almost every night. And when he didn't, I slid into his. He kept trying to get me to shimmy down the walls but I couldn't make myself do it, so finally he made this little half-pipe chute out of some scrap duct work he bought from a heating and cooling guy in the neighborhood. He put a wood frame around it to make it sturdier but it was still light enough for him to lift out of his window and lay on my sill without making too much noise. The drop wasn't all that steep so it was easy to climb back up by grabbing the outside of the wood frame. Frank was the tricky part. I knew I couldn't leave him behind or he'd start crying for me. He liked the slide down enough because I held him on my lap. But he couldn't get any traction going up and his claws made a real racket the first time we tried it. Then Jimmy got the idea of putting him in a laundry bag and tying some extra rope to the drawstring. I'd take the end with me when I climbed back, then pull Frank up behind me. He didn't like that much either but it worked. When I took him out of the bag he always looked around the room real confused, like he'd been beamed up there or something.

Sometimes Jimmy and I got stoned but mostly we just talked. And kissed a lot. Nothing more than that, at least not at first. He didn't push me to do other stuff and I guess I wasn't giving off any signals that I wanted to. I figured he had lots of experience and that kind of scared me. I mean I've told you I'm no tease or anything but those other guys I let do stuff to me were so clueless I always knew I was in control. With Jimmy, I was afraid if I waved him on to second he might try to stretch it into a triple or more and I wouldn't want to stop him. Plus he was the first really good kisser I ever made out with and there was something powerful about that. With everything on my mind, you, being away from Mom and Em and even David, Jimmy's kisses created this little force field around us that kept everything else away. Everything slowed down, just like being stoned, and an hour of making out with him could erase a whole day's worth of bad stuff. I think he must have felt a little bit the same. Jimmy had his share of things to try and block out.

When I asked him about the music that had nearly bounced me out of bed that first night he said he played that stuff because it was the only thing that sounded as angry as he felt. At first he was mostly mad at his mom for dying. Then when he started to love her again he got mad at everyone else for getting on with their lives without her.

His mom was much younger than his dad and they had five kids by the time she was twenty-seven and that was supposed to be it. Then the year she turned forty she started having these feelings and she thought she was having her life change early but it turned out to be Jimmy. She had all kinds of complications during the pregnancy and the birth, and Jimmy's dad told him she was never really the same after he was born. Jimmy said well, then, she really must have been something else before. When she was fifty she started having weird feelings down there again but knew it was different this time. It was cancer and she was dead a little more than a year later. Jimmy was ten.

We were in his room when he told me that. We hadn't kissed at all that night. He just started talking the minute I slid in, like I was late and he needed to catch me up. He didn't cry or anything. Maybe it had been too long. But he seemed anxious for me to know about her and I envied him being able to talk about her like that when I couldn't even tell him you'd ever existed.

"She sang to me every night," he told me. "I don't remember a single night of my entire life that didn't end with her voice. Even at the end when she couldn't come to my room anymore, she made me come to her and lie down with her and she'd sing in this whisper, always the same song."

He said his Dad wasn't built to be alone and he got remarried less than two years later. He said he felt like they both became his stepparents that day, like he was mostly a job that came with their new relationship. His stepmom seemed so weak compared to his mom. She liked to be taken care of and even though she wasn't young anymore, she was enough younger than his dad that he took on that role for her. All his brothers and sisters were long gone, some married with kids, and Jimmy was stuck watching his dad be in love with someone that wasn't his mom. That's when he started carrying her picture, stopped being mad at her and started in on everyone else. His brothers and sisters mostly had their own families and his mom's dying hardly seemed like a blip in their lives. At least to him. And even though the doctors said there was no connection between his mom's late pregnancy and the cancer, Jimmy always felt like his father blamed him. Then Jimmy started getting in trouble.

"It just gave him a good excuse to send me away, pay to let it be someone else's problem," Jimmy told me.

I said it seemed like an awful lot of money to pay if you didn't care about someone.

He said if I wanted to be on his dad's side I could go downstairs and wake him up.

I said I wasn't talking about sides, just if you were going to be mad at your own dad you should make sure of your reasons. I said maybe you'd like it better if you could buy your drugs from your dad instead of mine.

He said, "Okay, Tess DeNunzio. Settle down."

That was the only time we came close to fighting about anything and he seemed to look at me differently after that. More like we were equals and I was someone he could not only tell stuff to but ask about things too. Out of all the other things I liked about him, I think that's what made me start to fall in love with him.

At first we were only together at night but then Jimmy got me a summer job at Kennywood at the Thelma's Lemonade stand. It was right by the big final drop on the Logjammer ride and Jimmy worked right across from me at the Skycoaster. He worked at the park every summer and knew some people and they hired me and paid me cash even though I wasn't sixteen yet. Anyway, Thelma's is that really cold slushy lemonade and the funnest part about working there was watching people almost faint from brain freeze. They'd come to my stand all hot and sweaty, usually before getting in the long line for the Logjammer so they'd have something to keep them cool, and they'd take that first big gulp and get a look on their face like someone just put their head in a vise and turned it hard. "Man!" they'd say and shake their heads, and then tip the cup up for more. You'd think word would get around to go easy on that stuff at first but it was the same thing all day every day.

The Skycoaster where Jimmy worked was only the coolest ride there. You had to sign up and pay for it like three hours in advance and come back at your assigned time. Then they strapped you in three across in these harnesses that were attached to a bungee cord, hauled you up and back maybe a hundred and fifty feet and then made you pull the release cord yourself. At first it was just a free fall straight down, but then when the bungee caught it sent you screaming out over the lake and up over the Logjammer and my Thelma's stand. The Skycoaster and Thelma's and the Logjammer made up just about the busiest part of the park, especially when it was hot, and my days flew by. It seemed like time was kept by the screams from the Skycoaster and the bursts of water that came with every plunge down that last Logjammer hill, and Vicky taught me to time my conversations with our customers around those sounds.

Vicky was the girl who worked with me most days. She was a little horsey looking in the face but she had this killer body she wasn't afraid to show off that even made her buck teeth seem sexy. Guys were always crowded around our stand, ordering their Thelma's and drinking them right there, pushing stuff off the counter so Vicky'd have to bend over to pick it up. She knew what they were doing but she'd put on a real show for them anyway, letting her tank top fall away from her boobs or giving them a glimpse of her silk thong underwear sticking up out of the back of her tiny jean shorts. Sometimes Vicky would leave and "take a walk" with one of them for a while. It was her second summer there so she was a little loose about how she came and went but I didn't care. She took the stand while I had lunch with Jimmy almost every day, so she could hook up with whoever she wanted the rest of the day as far as I was concerned.

Working made the summer go fast and I felt a little bit like I'd started a new life or something. Now that school was over I never saw any of my friends. It was just me and my Dad and his family and Frank and Jimmy and now Vicky. Most days I had to be at the park by ten thirty to open my stand and just when the day seemed to get started it was already time for lunch with Jimmy. Usually we walked across the park to the Potato Patch, where they had the best fries I'd ever eaten. It was right under the Thunderbolt, this really fast old wooden roller coaster, and our lunchtime conversation weaved in and out of the coaster clattering over our heads. After lunch we'd wander back to the Logjammer and usually cut in line for a ride to cool off. Then I'd tap us both a free Thelma's and we'd sit and watch people's faces as they flew by on the Skycoaster. Jimmy said he never got tired of that. He said no matter how cool someone thinks they are, the first time they're pulling four Gs at the bottom of the arc, their faces show pure terror.

After lunch the long part of the day started. The park got crowded and the heat from the pavement was sometimes so heavy it seemed to hum. That's when Vicky would do most of her entertaining and leave most of the real work to me. I didn't care though. It gave me an excuse to ignore all those guys who even though some of them might have seemed cute to me before seemed pretty silly next to Jimmy. I'd be pulling Thelma's out of the tap almost non-stop until I was done at six and then meet my Dad at the park entrance at six-thirty. He was usually coming back from the gym, so he was starving and we'd grab a bite to eat or get takeout for home. After dinner my Dad usually made a few deliveries, had a few beers and fell asleep on the couch. Once he was out I'd tap on Jimmy's window, spend a few hours with him, sleep 'til nine and then the whole routine started over again. Everything was so new and my days were so full I didn't have time to think about everything else until I pulled Frank into bed with me, and by then I was so tired it didn't matter.

It was at least two weeks before Jimmy got me to go on the Skycoaster with him. He rode it all by himself every night he worked late, after closing time. The park was dark and quiet and he said it made him feel like a bat, soaring and free and dangerous. It was that last part that concerned me.

"The *ride's* not dangerous, Tess. It just makes you *feel* dangerous."

"Either way, no thanks."

"Come on, I've ridden that thing at least two hundred times. Do I look any worse for it?"

125

"I don't know. I didn't know you before."

"Look, I'm not going to make you do it, but you'd love it. I promise."

"Maybe another day."

"At least stay and watch me then. You can't get up your courage watching all these amateurs all day."

So sometimes I'd stay. My Dad had given me a cell phone when I started working and I'd call and tell him I was helping out at the Potato Patch until closing to make some extra money. He didn't really like me staying so late but the park was a safe place. I think mostly he didn't like having to wait until eleven to have his first beer.

Jimmy loved flying stoned so I'd smoke a little with him beforehand, being careful not to go past where I couldn't fake being straight with my Dad. But one night I got a little carried away and the extra buzz made me brave.

We were smoking and snuggling on the raised platform in the middle of the lake when I told him, "I'm going up with you tonight, Jimmy."

He pulled me in close then took the joint away from me. "That's my girl!" he said. "No more weed for you, though. I want you to feel it! Hey, Mickey!" He called to the other guy who worked the coaster with him. "Two going up!"

Mickey walked out to the platform and started buckling us into the harnesses. It was a warm night but I started shivering like crazy and probably would have chickened out if Mickey hadn't worked so fast. Once he'd clipped us in he helped us lock arms and that's when Jimmy could feel me shaking.

"Easy, Tess."

*"I can't do it! I can't, I can't!"*

But we were already on our way up.

I screamed, "*No! No!*" and closed my eyes and we went up and up and I thought we'd never stop. I could tell when we cleared the trees because the wind picked up and we started to sway. I dug my nails into Jimmy's arms. "Make it stop! I want to get off!"

"Too late. Open your eyes, Tess. Look at this!"

"*I can't!*" We were still going up. It felt impossible, like we were attached to a cloud instead of the steel pole I'd looked at every day, up and up.

"Tess, I'm not pulling the release until you open your eyes."

We had stopped with a jolt that brought my stomach into my throat and now we were swaying in complete silence like two fish at the end of a giant pole.

"*Good! Don't pull it! Mickey! Let us down!*"

"He's not going to do that, Tess, so you can either open your eyes or we can stay just like this for the rest of the night."

"*You're an ASSHOLE!*"

"Shh. Sound really carries from up here."

"*JIMMY FREEZE IS A GIANT ASSHOLE!*"

He was quiet for so long after that it was almost like he wasn't there anymore. There was just this soft swishing sound of the air in my ears. Then when he finally spoke again I swear this is what he said.

"Tess. I love you. Open your eyes."

"What?"

"Open your eyes."

"No. The other thing."

My stomach had started to settle and the rocking, locked together like that, felt really nice all of a sudden.

"I love you."

"You do?"

"Yeah."

"How do you know?"

"I don't know. I just do."

"Me too."

"Yeah?"

"Yeah."

I opened my eyes and didn't look down but right at Jimmy Freeze.

"No worries," he said and released us and we dropped weightless together into the night.

# *Mom*

After David asked I called Mom more often, at least twice a week. It was hard because I thought I was starting to feel better but she seemed just the same. Our calls got shorter and we talked about less and less important stuff until it was like I was calling some old aunt I never saw to thank her for the puzzle map of the United States she sent me for Christmas. There were these long silences while both of us tried to think of what to say next. I think it was because we never talked about you. You were this sort of hum in the background that made it hard to concentrate.

Then a few weeks before my sixteenth birthday I was telling her about Frank, how he was getting these skinny deer legs and pumped-up paws and she laughed a little bit and said it sounded like me a few years ago. After that she got real quiet but it wasn't the kind of quiet that felt like she didn't know what to say. Instead it felt like one of those times she was trying not to say something she wished she could say.

I said, "What, Mom?"

She said, "Nothing."

I said, "No, really, Mom. What?"

She was quiet again. Then after a while she said, "Do you think you might come home for your birthday?"

This time I was the one who got quiet. Because it felt funny that I'd never even thought of that.

"I don't know, Mom."

"We could have a little party, just us. Your Dad could come too if you want. After all, it is an important birthday." She was talking real fast, like she'd rehearsed it and needed to say it all at once before she forgot. "Or we could do something bigger. Invite friends from school, maybe rent the pool for the night and get a DJ or something. Whatever you want. With something bigger like that we could have all the space we needed and Em could have a couple of friends too. She's already made a card for you and she asked me whether she should send it or if she'd be able to give it to you, so I promised I'd ask. Next time we talked."

After a while I said, "I don't know, Mom."

"Well."

"I mean, thanks. That's really nice."

"Whatever you want. That's all I meant to say."

"Thanks."

"Okay then."

She was quiet again and I could tell this time she was trying not to cry. This happened a lot but she usually just pre-tended to cough or something and then thought up something else to talk about. This time she said what she must have been thinking all those other times.

"I can't lose both of you," she said softly. "I can't."

"No, Mom."

"I just can't, Tess. I wouldn't know what to do. I don't know what to do."

"You're not losing me, Mom."

"We're flying apart. All of us. Like something exploded in the middle of us." She was crying now and not trying to hide it from me. "We love each other, Tess. Don't we? All of us? Isn't that supposed to help? Why isn't it helping? Why are we running from each other? I mean, not just you. All of us."

"I don't know."

"Nothing happened, you know."

"Mom."

"With Justin."

"Mom, I told you. That's not why I . . ."

"Nothing happened. He was just someone, I don't know. He was just someone who wasn't you or David or Em. He was someone I could talk to, even laugh with, without feeling guilty about actually feeling good for a few minutes, you know? Do you know what I mean, Tess?"

I thought about Jimmy. "Yeah, Mom. I do."

"He just thought it was going to be something it wasn't. And maybe I let him think that because I didn't want to lose those few minutes of forgetting every once in a while."

"It's okay, Mom."

"No it isn't. You're there and I'm here. That's never been okay. That's never been. It's always been you and me, Tess. Remember when it was just you and me?"

I put my hand over the phone for a few seconds because I did remember, and that made me start to cry with her.

"Yeah, Mom."

"You were my best friend, you know? Even before you could talk. There was no one else anymore, once you were born. Your father, all my friends, they all seemed so silly after you. I went from being a stupid kid one day to seeing I was surrounded by stupid kids the next. You were the only important thing, the only thing I could never lose, and now I'm losing you."

"No, Mom."

"Yes. I am. I can feel it."

"No, Mom. I promise."

We were quiet for a while, both of us, I think, wondering what I was promising. I didn't know, but I didn't feel like I was lying either.

"I always knew you might run to your father someday. I just never thought it would be for stability." She laughed a little and sniffled. "God, I'm such a wreck. I don't blame you."

"Don't worry, Mom."

"Okay. Okay then."

That was the closest we came to talking about you the whole time I was gone. And even though you were what we should have been talking about, I couldn't help but be glad we were talking about me instead.

## You & Em

Something that first doctor, Miss Soothing, kept trying to get me to admit was that maybe I was a little bit jealous of you. And Em too. That since you weren't my full sisters and since you took a lot of attention away from me that I maybe felt isolated in my own family. She said the only way to deal with my guilt was to recognize that it might have a source beyond your death itself.

I never felt that way. Never.

I did get lonely for Mom sometimes though. She was so busy with you and Em that I got every teenage girl's wish: I was left alone. I don't mean I was neglected or anything, but when I closed my door it stayed closed. You or Em might come knocking but I think Mom thought of my need for privacy as a gift to her. I was one thing she didn't have to worry about anymore. And for the most part that was okay with me. But sometimes I wanted her to myself again.

I never had a babysitter when I was a kid. Mom hardly ever

went anywhere before we met David, and when she did she always took me with her. None of her friends even had kids, so I think I was sort of a novelty to them. If there was a party, I was invited too. I was sort of like Mom's mascot. After we met David it was mostly the same thing. He understood that he was dating a package. Since Mom worked back then our time together didn't start until she picked me up at day care at around six o'clock, so she kept me up late to play games or watch TV shows I was way too young for. When I think about it now I realize David must have been dying for me to go to bed so he could get romantic with Mom. But I don't remember him ever trying to rush the process. He just became part of our routine.

Once you and Em came along, that all changed. Mom stopped working but it seemed like she was more tired than when she did work. They needed time to be alone together once in a while, Mom and David, and I was just getting old enough to babysit so that worked out perfectly. I got to make some money for clothes and stuff and I got time alone with you. I complained about it sometimes but I loved it. I never resented you. What I resented was Mom not choosing to spend any of her free time with me. I only wanted to be left alone until I was, if that makes any sense.

But as for you and Em, you were always my sisters, never less, and sometimes more. Maybe it was the age difference. Sometimes when Mom and David went out and we would play house and Em would make me the mom, that's how I felt. Like you were my little girls. When Mom and David first got married, I prayed for you—literally prayed, between my Dad and my Gram in their old Catholic church—prayed for sisters. And when it didn't happen right away I remember telling Mom that Amy Bregar had sisters and maybe Amy's mom knew something she didn't and could help her. And when Mom did finally get pregnant with Em, and when we all went to the hospital together for the sonogram and I watched the nurse spread the clear jelly on Mom's stomach and then watched the screen, my eyes crossing from Em coming in and out of view, and the nurse asking if we wanted to know the sex and Mom and I smiling at each other and nodding and David putting his hand on my head, and the nurse saying you couldn't ever be one hundred percent sure with little girls but this sure looked like one, I already knew. I knew that my first sister was coming and that I was going to be part of a family.

And whatever the psychology books say about what kids like me are supposed to feel, I never stopped feeling that way. Never.

# Travis Chills Out

We had a hot spell late in July when it got up into the high nineties every day for almost a whole week, which meant it was about a hundred and ten on the pavement in the park. It was that really heavy wet heat like they get in the south that people up here aren't used to, where you feel like you're walking through baby oil. No one wanted to be outside, so the crowds at the park really thinned out, even my corner where people came to cool off. I know it was just because we weren't busy but it seemed like the air slowed the days down too. Vicky and I spent most of our time sitting in the one shaded corner of our booth or trading off rides on the Logjammer, which helped for about five minutes until the water boiled off our bodies and got replaced by sweat again. The park was a totally different place that week. Families stayed home, so it was all older kids, scraggly looking couples and packs of shirtless, tattooed boys. I left right at six-thirty every day and spent the evenings sitting in front of the window-unit air conditioner in my Dad's living room watching TV. I slept down there most nights too since there was AC in my Dad's bedroom but not mine, so I didn't see much of Jimmy after work that week either. I was pretty sure my Dad knew about Jimmy by then—not the nighttime stuff but that we hung out at the park together—but after I found out about his little "business" he didn't seem as interested in questioning my choice of friends.

On the hottest day of that week I got a visit from one of my Dad's own questionable choices. The pavement was sticky and the air was so heavy and still you could hardly move it with your own breath. Vicky had just come back from the Logjammer and was slumped in the shady corner trying to stay wet and I was tapping about my sixth Thelma's of the day when I heard his voice. I recognized it but not fast enough to tell Vicky to take care of this one for me and when I turned around Travis was already holding his money out to me.

He looked like a dead body that had been dug up. He had no shirt on and his jeans sagged real low under his little pot belly. Skin just sort of hung off the rest of him and he slouched like he was walking downhill.

He said, "Hey Tess. How 'bout a cold one for an old friend?"

I said, "Okay. You want one too?"

"Heh. You're a funny one. Like your old man. You still samplin' the inventory? Your Dad's I mean." He put an imaginary joint to his thin lips, sucked in and smiled. His teeth looked like corn. He was very stoned.

I asked him, "Didn't you get enough last time, Travis?"

"That a threat?"

The shiner my Dad had given him had faded to a greenish-yellow bruise but it glowed with sweat and there was still a bro-

137

ken blood vessel in his eye. It was all teary in the heat. Vicky was familiar enough with trouble to know when it showed up for a Thelma's and she stood up to help. Travis didn't even pretend not to look her up and down.

"Who's your friend?" he said.

"No one. What size do you want, Travis?"

"Depends on what sizes you're offerin' little lady." He said it to me but he was still looking at Vicky. She baited him too. She was still wet from the Logjammer and her T-shirt clung to her like she'd been in one of those MTV Spring Break contests.

She said, "I don't know about you but I think the bigger the better." She moved her hips and said it real sexy but mocking and anyone but someone like Travis in his current state would have known they were about to get taken for a ride.

"I bet you do," he said.

Vicky said, "You like what you see?"

"Oh yeah."

"How big do you think you can handle?"

"I think that's a better question for you." Travis put his thumbs in his pockets and let them pull his jeans down even further until you could see the very beginning of the line of black hair that attached his white crotch to his white belly. I wanted to puke.

Vicky said, "Think you can handle this?" She made a show of bending over to get one of the thirty-two-ounce souvenir cups out of the box under our counter and when she straightened she held it up and sort of brushed it across her boobs. Travis looked like a dog being made to sit for his dinner.

He said, "Yeah, that looks just about my size, fit me like a one-fingered glove."

"'Cause we're running a little contest just to keep a slow day interesting," Vicky said.

"You the prize?"

"Could be."

Travis kept smiling with his eyes half closed, trying to act sexy, but it just made him look more stoned. "Go ahead. I'm game," he said.

"For today and today only, anyone who can chug one of these Big Thelma's in ten seconds or less gets a ride with one of us on The Olde Mill."

The Olde Mill was one of those ancient boat rides through a bunch of dark tunnels and supposedly scary scenes no one's even looking at because they're too busy making out. I knew what she was up to now but I pretended to be shocked.

"Vicky!" I said, real loud and exaggerated.

"Quit worryin', girl. I wouldn't pick you anyway," Travis said. "Would we get a boat to ourselves?"

"Just you and the lady of your choice."

"What're the rules once we get in there?"

"I'm not aware of any rules." Vicky was good at this. If she hadn't been talking to Travis I would have believed her. "Just finish what you're doing before the light at the end of the tunnel."

"Fill 'er up girl!" Travis said.

Vicky turned to the Thelma's dispenser and pulled the valve. She didn't have to bend over but she stuck her butt out anyway and wiggled it. When the cup was full she turned to Travis, stuck a finger in it, then slid her finger into her mouth slow and easy and pulled it back out the same way. A big drop of sweat rolled into Travis's bad eye and he winked it hard.

Vicky said, "I don't have a second hand, Tess. You got one?"

"Yep, got it." I held my wrist up level with my eyes.

"Okay now, Travis. It's Travis, right? When Tess says one two three go, you got ten seconds."

"You don't know who you're dealin' with, honey. I can do a pitcher of Bud in less than that."

Vicky smiled at him real sweet. "I don't mind telling you Thelma's is a little tougher than beer. At least for me."

"Gimme that thing."

"Here you go. Wait for Tess."

I looked at my watch. "One, two, three, go!"

I have to give Travis credit. I wasn't even looking at my watch but he gulped that thing down pretty quick. And he stayed standing longer than I would have thought. Then the king of all brain freezes hit him like two wrecking balls from either side of his skull and he was down on the pavement holding his head and screaming.

"*Aawwwwwwk!*"

Vicky said, "Twelve seconds. So close, Travis."

"*Aawwwkk. Fuck!*"

"You can try again if you want."

He started to get his voice back a little but he was still holding his head.

"Fuckin' bitch DeNunzio! I'll fuckin' kill you!"

"Me? I was just the timer."

"I'll fuckin' kill both of you!"

Vicky said, "You dropped your souvenir cup, Travis. Don't forget to take it with you."

Jimmy must have heard the screaming from his platform because he was already on his way over by the time Travis was pulling himself to his feet. Travis managed to clear all the napkins and spoons and straws off our counter with his forearm before Jimmy got him under the armpits from behind.

Jimmy said, "Travis, I never figured you for a Thelma's man."

I said, "You know him?"

"From the neighborhood."

"Get the fuck off me Freeze!"

"No one ever learns. Gotta watch that first sip."

"Fuckin' bitches almost killed me!" He was still squeezing his eyes shut like he was trying to blow bubbles through his ears.

"Okay, Travis. Chalk it up as one for the bad guys. Now move your sorry ass so I don't have to call Security."

"On me? What the fuck I do?"

Jimmy slid one hand down over a little lump in Travis's pocket. "Maybe they wouldn't call the cops over that little bit, but you never know. You still on parole?"

Travis shook free, but only because Jimmy let him.

"Fuck all of you," he said, but the fight was pretty much out of him.

When he was gone, I said to Jimmy what a pitiful excuse for a human being that Travis was. Jimmy said maybe so but watch out for him anyway. Then Vicky and I closed up early and went home. We didn't even ask.

# The Whip

One day not too long after that I was walking back from lunch with Jimmy and I saw David and Em. Jimmy and I had gotten a little stoned, so it almost felt like I sensed them before I even saw them. I was passing through this section of the park called "Lost Kennywood" where they put all the old rides no one would go on anymore except that putting them all together made them seem special somehow—The Salt & Pepper Shakers, The Swings, The Turtles—and something made me look over at The Whip when I was passing it. There were a lot of kids with their parents and most of the kids got real wide eyes going around the corners, their heads snapping back and their hair going straight out, then they'd laugh the whole way down the straightaway until the whip sucked the air out of them again.

I recognized David from behind. He was moving away from me and at first it looked like he was riding by himself because Em was still so little her head didn't go above the back of the seat. David's arm was around her though, and when they hit the corner and Em came into view, you could see her whole body just kind of press into his. The only clue that she was moving at all was the bill of her flowered cap tipped back a little every time. She's so different from you on rides. She didn't laugh down the straightaways or anything. She just looked like she was concentrating to get ready for the next whip. I could tell she was having fun though.

It felt weird seeing them there, like they'd crossed over into this other world I'd created for myself. I didn't wave to them or try to get their attention or anything, and I didn't really mean for them to see me. But everything was moving all slow from the weed, like a slide show instead of a movie, and in one slide they were coming off the ride and then in the next one they were standing practically right in front of me before I could even think to move my feet.

David said, "Tess?"

"Hey." I was answering David but I was looking at Em, who had an arm around one of his legs and was looking at the ground. I hadn't seen her since her last day of school.

"Hey Em, look who's here! What are you doing here, Tess?"

"Working."

"You work here?"

"Yeah."

"Does your mother know that?"

"I'm not sure if I told her."

"I thought you had to be sixteen?"

"I have a friend."

"Oh."

While David and I were talking Em just kept looking down.

David said, "You look tired. Are you okay?"

"Yeah, I'm fine. Just really hot."

"So where do you work?"

"At the Thelma's stand. Over by the Logjammer."

"We were just headed over there to cool off, weren't we Em?"

Em didn't look up.

"I'm sort of on a break right now."

"Oh. Okay. Maybe later."

"Yeah. Stop by a little later. Okay, Em?" She nodded but didn't look at me. "I'll let you get your own Thelma's from the machine. Maybe you can even stay a while and help me serve some people."

"That's sounds fun, huh Em?" David put his hand on her head, then moved it down and rubbed her ear.

"I'm not thirsty."

"Well. Maybe later."

We stood like that, the three of us, not saying anything. When we were talking I could push the buzz aside but standing silent brought it back and stretched everything out so it felt like some angry Greek god had turned us all into statues in Lost Kennywood.

"She's better," David finally said. "Your mother's getting better."

"Good."

"I wish she were here now."

"How come she's not?"

"Too hot for her. You know your mother. Eighty's too hot, seventy's too cold."

"Yeah."

"We're meeting her for dinner though. If you'd like to come."

"I've got plans. With friends."

"Okay. Maybe next time."

"Yeah. Next time."

"She would have come, you know. If she'd known you'd be here, she'd have come no matter what."

"Tell her I'll call her soon, okay."

"Sure."

"I'll call soon, Em. Maybe we can talk too." She had put a few strands of hair into the corner of her mouth and part of her cheek was between her teeth.

We said good-bye and David said they'd see me later at Thelma's but I wasn't sure Em would want to. When they were walking away from me I could see David trying to kid Em out of her funk. Her neck's real ticklish and he poked a finger into the side of it and her head flopped sideways real fast and trapped his finger. Then he pushed her cap down over her eyes and grabbed her under the arms and put her up on his shoulders. The further away they got from me the harder it was to tell where David stopped and Em began, like they were just one tall person. But not a whole person. There was still a part missing from both of them, a part I'd helped take away and couldn't put back. And no matter how long I stayed away from them that would still be true.

I went back to my stand and told Vicky I wasn't feeling so great from the heat and she said it was no problem if I left early. So I'm not sure if Em and David stopped by or not.

# Fast-Forward

Once the heat broke, the summer started moving so fast it was like August was a downhill part of the calendar and I was sliding toward the anniversary. I passed a newsstand on August 7 and the front page of the *New York Times* said: "New York to Observe Sept. 11 with Dawn-to-Dusk Tributes." On the news they talked about what they might do, who would be there, and all those news magazine shows did pieces on the families, how they were getting through the year, how they would mark the day, how they would go on from here. I stopped watching television because there weren't any shows about people like us. The country was fighting the War on Terror. Little crimes like mine didn't matter anymore. Little deaths like yours didn't make a sound.

My Dad disappeared more and more often in the evenings, sometimes taking the truck, sometimes not, sometimes saying he was going to the gym, sometimes not bothering to pretend.

By early August the Pirates were a lost cause and his attention, when he was home, shifted to Steelers' training camp. David and Em never came back to the park but it was almost like they never left because I found myself looking for them all the time. Vicky went from one guy to the next, usually overlapping, and there were two fistfights over her right in front of us. She laughed both times. Gallons and gallons of Thelma's got tapped and drunk, and Jimmy and I flew through cooler and cooler nights on the Skycoaster until I could feel the fine hair on my arms rising up to meet the breeze. Vicky asked if I was "doing him" yet because if I wasn't someone else was going to, and I didn't talk to her for days until she made me believe she wasn't talking about herself.

Mom was sounding better on the phone, more like herself, and I started looking forward to our calls. I worried more and more about Em though. Mom told me she was refusing to go to second grade because Miss Ellenbogen had gotten married and moved to Ohio. When Mom explained to her that she wouldn't have had Miss Ellenbogen again anyway Em said of course she knew that, but what were they teaching her that Mom didn't know and couldn't show her at home anyway? And how did she know her new teacher wouldn't just leave in the middle of the year, since everyone was always leaving? I asked Mom to put Em on the phone but Em said she was busy. Mom said my school schedule had come too and when I didn't say anything and she didn't push me on it, I couldn't decide if I was grateful for that or not.

I fell harder in love with Jimmy every day, partly because it felt so good to let myself do that, to feel something so extreme that wasn't sadness. And he never acted afraid. He just kept accepting it, as if he expected everything I said or did and he was just waiting for it to happen and saying, "What took you so long, Tess?" During that time, I found myself thinking that this was the best summer of my life. But it was hard to feel right about that.

# Sixteen

On August 21, a day before my sixteenth birthday, my Dad used his one phone call from the police station to tell me *not* to call my Mom. He said to call Gram instead and have her come over and stay with me because he thought he'd be out in less than a day since he didn't even have anything on him when they picked him up. He was just part of one of those big sweeps where they pick up everyone they have any information on. He said he saw Travis's face in the backseat of one of the police cars, which was going to be too bad for Travis pretty soon. I could tell he didn't really want me to call Gram since he'd never want her to find out. He was just saying to call her if I didn't think I'd be okay alone for one night, so I said, "Don't worry about it, Dad, I'll be okay," and I figured I'd tap on Jimmy's window and then my Dad said, "Hey Tess?"

"Yeah?"

He said, "Jimmy's here too."

I was quiet for a while.

Then I said, "He was with you?"

"Yeah."

So that's how I found out how Jimmy really knew my Dad and why my Dad didn't want me hanging around with him. I felt pretty stupid. Not betrayed or anything because I knew they both were mostly looking out for me. But I felt really young to need to be protected that way and really stupid not to have figured it out. It seems like I never figure things out. Stuff just happens to me and then I see how I should have seen it coming. I hope that changes when you get to be an adult. I don't want to live my whole life afraid of what's going to happen next.

It was really weird being home alone that night. Even though my Dad had been out a lot lately, the house never felt empty when I knew he was coming home. Watching TV and getting ready for bed knowing I was going to be by myself made everything feel quiet. I was moving around and doing things just to kill time, not because I really wanted to be doing them. Frank must have sensed it too, or maybe he could just tell I was acting strange, because he followed me around panting even though it wasn't hot, and whenever I looked at him he moved his eyebrows all over the place like he was waiting for me to answer a question he'd just asked. I started to see why old people who lived alone talked to their dogs. I kept telling him, "It's okay buddy. Daddy'll be home tomorrow," but I was mostly talking to myself.

In bed it was even worse. I don't think it would have been so bad if my Dad had been anywhere else, but thinking about him in jail, and Jimmy there with him, made it feel like I had been part of everything but didn't know it until they got caught. You couldn't go fifteen minutes without hearing a siren somewhere around my Dad's neighborhood and even though I was used to them, it all of a sudden felt like they were coming for me, the last member of the DeNunzio family drug ring, the one who knew everything, or would if she'd just look once in a while. Frank was no help. He kept getting up and lying down in different spots, at my feet, curled behind my knees, on the floor, and finally next to my pillow and breathing right in my face. I'd been talking to him all night and I asked him if he'd brushed his teeth and he turned his head away from me and curled it into his own chest like he'd understood me and was insulted. And just when he got settled down, Keisha came wandering into my room looking for my Dad. She left and came back about every twenty minutes until two o'clock in the morning when she finally jumped up with me and Frank. Even though the heat wave was over, that's a lot of dog on a summer night, so I moved us all into my Dad's room with the window-unit AC.

That seemed to calm the dogs down but it made me even more wide awake. You might be surprised to know that my Dad keeps his room really neat but there's not much in it—just a big bed and a dresser with a mirror, and a bench press and some other weights lined up against the wall. So that makes the wedding picture on the dresser of him and Mom one of the only things to look at. Even when I closed my eyes that picture was the closest thing to another person in the house, so I could feel Mom watching me. Except it wasn't a comforting kind of thing—like she was watching over me—because in the picture she was just young and stupid like me, marrying a big strong guy mostly to get away from her stepdad and because Nick DeNunzio once told a whole gang who was about to attack him, "You ain't got enough guys." I had never thought of Mom like that before. Even when she told me that story, that's all it was. Just a story about someone who was nothing like her. But the longer she looked at me from that picture the more I could feel everything she was feeling when it was taken and I knew I was wrong before. She *didn't* know she was making a mistake. Only the Mom I know now would know that. The Mom in the picture is the happiest person I've ever seen. She thinks she is starting the rest of her life on that day, that she and my Dad will fill a house with children and that doing that and being together will change him and make him into someone who wants to succeed, who might learn computers or become a chef or open his own gym. Maybe that's why he keeps it. You wouldn't ever want to forget you made someone that happy once.

That finally made me tired, thinking about my parents like real people, and a little scared too. There aren't that many mistakes you can make when you're fifteen that change your whole life. But Mom was only a little more than two years older than me when she married my Dad and then I came along a year later. Mom never counts me as one of her mistakes but that's only because she doesn't think of me like that now. Back then I had to be. If it's a mistake to marry someone, doesn't it have to be a mistake to have a baby with him too? Anyway, I started to think about how I'm not that far away from being able to make those kinds of mistakes and it started to scare me. If my Dad still wasn't smart enough to keep a job and stay out of jail, what kinds of stupid things was I waiting to do? Maybe even coming to live with him was one of them. It didn't feel like it, but what kind of guarantee was that when Mom was looking at me from that picture so sure of herself?

I fell asleep thinking about that and I had a dream that I was your mother. And Em's too. I was in Em's first grade room handing out cupcakes for her birthday treat. Miss Ellenbogen was still Miss Ellenbogen but she was pregnant and while the kids are all eating their cupcakes she says to me, "Don't you have another daughter?" and all of a sudden I can't breathe and I go running out to the parking lot, except it's like I'm running in clear syrup and I can't find my car because I don't remember what it looks like or even learning how to drive. Then all of a sudden there aren't any cars except mine and it's right next to me and I look in and there you are, still strapped in your car seat, safe. Everything speeds back up and the air is normal and I can breathe again. And then I open the car door and see that you aren't quite right. Someone has drugged you or something. You don't even move right away and when you finally turn to look at me, your eyes can't focus and there are two thin lines of blood coming out of your nose. I scream and reach for you but then I start yelling that it's all your fault. That you are a big girl now and can unbuckle yourself and why didn't you follow us in and didn't you see all the things Mommy had to carry in to the party? And when you don't even look at me because you can't, I get even angrier and slam the car door closed.

Then I wake up and I am sixteen.

153

It was the phone next to my Dad's bed that woke me up. I don't know how many times it rang before I heard it and I had to climb across Keisha to answer it. It was my Dad.

He said, "Hey, Tess. You okay?"

"Yeah."

"Sorry. I wake you up?"

"Yeah."

"Sorry."

"It's okay."

"I mean about everything."

"Dad, it's okay."

"No, it ain't. This ain't worth a few extra bucks. I'm done with it."

"That's good."

"I was tellin' Jimmy, I'm thinkin' about cooking school again."

I had heard this before. "That's great, Dad."

"Or maybe coaching. Like a strength coach or something. I mean I was thinkin', who knows more about that stuff than me?"

"No one, Dad."

"I'm serious."

"I know. That'd be great."

I was looking at the picture again while we talked and realized I never really noticed much about my Dad in it, except how much hair he had. He looks just as happy as Mom but it's more than that. He looks like he really wants to be the person she thinks she's marrying.

I asked him, "Are you coming home?"

"Yeah. Me and Jimmy have to go get the truck outa hock. We should be there by lunchtime."

"Okay."

"Is Gram there?"

"No."

"How come?"

"I didn't call her. It was just one night. And I had the dogs."

"Thanks. Really, thanks."

"No worries, Dad."

"Okay, then. We'll see you soon."

"See you soon, Dad."

I was just about to hang up and then I heard whispering in the background that sounded like Jimmy and then my Dad said, "Jesus, Tess, happy birthday!"

"Thanks."

"We'll do somethin' special, I promise."

"Sounds great."

"Jesus, sixteen!"

"Yep."

"Somethin' special tonight. Just you and me. And Jimmy if you want."

"Okay."

"Bye, Tess."

"Bye."

"Happy birthday."

∞

After breakfast I called my boss at Kennywood and told him I couldn't get a ride to work and then Frank and I went out onto the porch. It was clear and cool, more like September than August, except you could feel it was going to warm up fast. Even my Dad's neighborhood didn't look so bad in that soft light.

I guess I shouldn't have been surprised to see Mom's car pull up to the curb but I was. When she got out I felt like I had been sitting there waiting for her to pick me up after my first half day of kindergarten, that's how happy I was to see her. She had on a simple sleeveless white top and black shorts and her arms and legs were even a little bit tan. Her hair was pulled back in a ponytail and she was wearing sunglasses and the silver hoop earrings I had picked out for David to give her two Christmases ago. From far away she looked like someone's babysitter or a college girl home for the summer. She pulled a small shopping bag from the other front seat and waved it and called up to me.

"Happy birthday!"

Frank ran down to greet her and she stooped down to his level.

"Oh, is this Frank? He's beautiful! You're so beautiful! Look at those eyes! Come on, boy." She waved him along with her and as soon as she got close enough she kissed me on the cheek from halfway down the steps and gave me a quick hug like she visited me every day. Then she sat down and started fishing around inside the bag. All of her movements were rushed and I could tell she wasn't sure whether or not I wanted her there so she was trying not to make a big deal out of it. But after the night I'd had I was wishing she *would* make a big deal out of it, and seeing her made me miss her all of a sudden, if that makes any sense. I wanted her to back up and start again so I could go running down the steps with Frank and let her wrap me up and hold me so tight I'd have to hold my breath until she let go.

But the moment had passed and I had missed it because I hadn't seen it coming, just like always. Who wouldn't figure that their Mom would want to see them on their sixteenth birthday? Me, that's who.

She was still rummaging through the bag, which I thought was strange because there weren't that many things in it. And then she sniffed once and I could see that her eyes were wet behind her sunglasses.

She kept looking into the bag and said, "Aren't you going to say anything?"

"Sorry."

What I wanted to say was that with all the things I was thinking I didn't even realize I hadn't said anything yet, but I couldn't think of the right way to say that. Not fast enough anyway.

"That's okay. I shouldn't have surprised you like this. But I was afraid if I called you'd tell me not to come, and I couldn't have that."

"No, Mom, it's okay. I would've told you to come."

She took off her sunglasses and wiped her eyes with the back of her hand. Up close you could see the little lines on her face and the freckling on her chest and shoulders that might tell you she could be someone's mom, but you'd still never think she was old enough to be mine.

"Where's your father?"

"At the gym," I lied.

"Really? It's not even breakfast time for him yet. Is he turning over a new leaf?"

"Sort of." Which was true. "You know, he got me to school every day."

"I know. And that was really great of him. I don't mean to be critical."

We didn't say anything for a minute.

Then she said, "So you start next week, right? School, I mean."

"Yeah. I guess."

"Did you get the summer reading list I sent over?"

"Yeah."

"Which ones did you pick?"

"I didn't really get started yet."

"Don't you think you better . . . Never mind."

"No, Mom. You're right. I better. I just haven't yet."

"Will your father be taking you again?"

"I guess."

Frank was sitting between us and looking back and forth while we talked. He seemed to understand that he wasn't the center of attention just then. Mom still hadn't taken anything out of the bag and she looked away from me, down the street toward the big smokestack.

"Where's Em?" I asked her.

"With David. I told her I was running an errand. I didn't want her to see you here and then think of you here."

"Why not?"

"I don't know. She likes Nick, and even though it's hard for her, at least she can think of you with him, but not here."

"She's just a kid, Mom. She wouldn't know the difference. I never did before."

"I know. But things happen here. I never liked you coming. Even just overnight. It's never safe here."

"It's never safe anywhere, Mom."

She nodded but didn't look at me. When she did turn she said, "So, should we open our presents?"

"Sure."

"It's not much. Just a few little things. I didn't want you to think I was trying to bribe you with gifts."

"Mom."

"Here." She handed me the bag.

Most of my friends ask for money for their birthdays since their parents don't have a clue what to get them. Maybe it's because Mom's younger but I almost always like what she picks out, even clothes. She didn't bring a lot—a couple of tank tops from Abercrombie, some of my apricot face scrub, and a really cool sterling silver thumb ring—but I could tell she'd spent a lot of time thinking about everything. The presents gave us something to talk about and we got more comfortable with each other, and pretty soon I was telling her stuff we never talked about on the phone, Kennywood and Vicky and even Jimmy. Obviously, I left out the part about crawling through each other's windows almost every night. Mom is cool but there are limits.

Before I knew it we had talked for more than an hour and when she asked when I was expecting my Dad I all of a sudden got paranoid that he was going to be home any minute. I started saying things to try and get her out of there because I didn't want my Dad coming home and thinking I'd called her, and then him spill the beans about what had happened without meaning to. But at the same time I didn't want her to leave. Maybe it was because I'd just spent the night alone but I felt so safe with her. I wanted her to pull me into her lap like I was Em's age again and curl my head under her chin, but it felt like a million years since we'd done that together and I didn't know how to start.

"So," I said. "I gotta go to work pretty soon."

"Oh. Alright. Can I give you a ride?"

"No, that's okay. Jimmy should be here any minute."

"That's great. Then I'll get to meet him."

"No. I don't think today would be such a good day."

"Why not?"

"I don't know. I've told him so much about you and he's kind of nervous about meeting you. He's real shy even normally, but meeting you is something he would sort of need some warning about."

I could tell she didn't believe me. Mom's not stupid. But she also didn't want to argue with me under the circumstances, so she ruffled Frank's head and we both stood up. Then she hugged me and this time we both held on for a long time.

"I love you so much, Tess. You know that."

"Yes."

"And I want you to come home. You know that too."

"Yes, I do."

"Okay then."

When we let go she looked like she didn't know what to do with her hands. She put them in her pockets and walked down the steps and to her car that way. She waved once before getting in. Then she was gone.

So here's another thing I should have seen coming. Frank and I are still out on the porch waiting for my Dad. I've gone inside and made myself an ice cream cone and I'm sitting on the steps sharing it with Frank. Other than his paws, his tongue is the fastest growing thing on him and he practically pushes the scoops right off the cone when it's his turn. He's hilarious because he closes his eyes and kind of moans from way down in his chest while he's licking the ice cream, like he can't believe how lucky he is.

He's right in the middle of a lick when the truck comes around the corner and his eyes pop open and his ears go straight up at the same time. I only have one hand to try and grab him because the other one feels like it needs to hold on to the ice cream and he slips me pretty easily and stumbles down the steps. He greets the truck all the time so I'm not too worried, except he's really frantic this time, and when I look up I can see the two men I love most in the world looking at each other and arguing about something. My Dad has one hand on the wheel and the other keeps pointing at Jimmy. Jimmy has both hands in the air, palms up. Behind them, bouncing off the ceiling, is a huge bunch of balloons, pink and white. It's different than it was with you because there's sound. I can hear my own scream, even if my Dad and Jimmy don't in time. I can hear Frank's toenails trying to scratch to a stop and the thud of the right front bumper against the side of his head and the high yelp that comes out in the split second before the impact silences him. I can hear my own footsteps slapping the pavement and my Dad and Jimmy scrambling out of the truck. I can hear my Dad saying over and over again, *"Jesus, Tess, I'm sorry. I didn't see him. I didn't see him."* Down on the pavement, Frank's eyes are wide and scared and his tongue is hanging out but he's breathing, real fast and shallow.

My Dad scoops him up gently and lays him inside the truck on the floor. Before I can even tell him I need to come with him my Dad is putting the truck in gear. He knows what I'm thinking though because he says, "It's not gonna be safe ridin' in here. I'll call you as soon as I know anything." Then he says, "Stay with her, Jimmy" and he's gone, just like Mom.

# Little Dance

Jimmy and I went inside and he led me up the stairs to my room. It was the first time he'd ever come in through the door. We laid on my bed and he held me for a long time while I cried. When I stopped he asked if I'd be okay if he left for a minute. He went back down the stairs and out the front door and pretty soon I could hear him in his room through my window. When he came back he was holding a small package wrapped in tinfoil.

"Happy birthday," he said.

"Yeah. So far it's great."

"Maybe it'll get better." He handed the package to me. It didn't weigh anything. It just felt like a bunch of tinfoil folded up together. That made me smile for some reason.

"I didn't know the jail had a gift shop."

"I've had this for a couple days. I just had to wrap it. It's not much."

I held my hand out flat like a scale. "That's for sure."

"Open it."

Inside was a cloth bag made out of flowered material. The bag wasn't any bigger than my palm and it had a drawstring top. It felt like it was empty.

Jimmy said, "Look inside."

I worked my finger into the bunched up top and pulled it open. My fingers touched a narrow slip of paper that I would have thought was just a manufacturer's tag or something, except it seemed to be the only thing in there so I took it out.

"What's this, my fortune?"

"Sort of. Read it."

It said, "This is Tess DeNunzio's makeup case. It will hold all of the makeup she will ever need for the rest of her life."

I said, "Very funny."

He said, "Not meant to be," and he had this very serious look on his face.

"Thanks."

Then he smiled. "There's something else. I obviously put it in there before my encounter with the local authorities."

Tucked way down at the very bottom, along the seam, was a small joint rolled in pink paper. Along the side it said "Sweet Sixteen," real small.

He said he didn't suppose I felt much like getting stoned, and I said actually I'd never felt more like it in my entire life.

We moved to the windowsill and passed it back and forth for a while without saying much. I had gotten pretty good at taking long drags and holding the smoke all the way past where it burns to where it cools to the temperature of your lungs. When it does that you can feel the high move right up through your chest and neck to your head. And it always had the same effect on me, which I am sure is why he put it in there. I wanted to kiss Jimmy Freeze more than anything in the world.

I don't know why it went past that this time. But when Jimmy touched his fingers to my waist and started to lift my tank top over my head, it felt like we did that every time. I moved away from him and let him watch me while I took off my bra and then stepped out of my shorts. Then I watched him strip down to his underwear and we both just stood there smiling at each other. But then he got that real serious look on his face again and he pulled me to him and our skin from our legs all the way up to our mouths felt like it melted together where it touched. Then I was on my back in my bed, under the covers with Jimmy, and I didn't remember getting there. And for the first time in so long I wasn't thinking about anything, not you, not Mom, not Frank, not even what I was doing with my hands or my mouth, or what Jimmy was doing with his, because all that mattered was the feeling of what we were doing together.

And then Jimmy's face disappeared under the covers, and let me tell you he knew how to do the little dance and I lost myself and I stayed in that place where nothing bad had ever happened and Jimmy's mouth was I swear touching my soul because I had no body anymore and I don't know if it was Jimmy or the weed but the rush that started to come over me was like nothing I'd ever felt and was like going over a waterfall in the dark over and over again without ever hitting the bottom and I started to cry from it because all of a sudden it also became something I didn't deserve to be feeling, and when I pulled Jimmy's face up and away from me he must have thought I wanted him inside me now and he slid in so easily, not with the awkward force I'd always feared, so he was over me, rising up on his arms, before he could have ever known. And I opened to him while I cried because even if I didn't deserve to feel this, he did, and I could see in his face that he was in the place I had been before and I tried, I really tried, to get back there with him. But then the bed was going *bump-bump*, against the wall, a sound like a heartbeat but also the sound of the truck hitting Frank, the sound of the gurney carrying you over the threshold of the emergency room, your little body jumping as if shocked, bump-bump, and Jimmy suddenly felt red-hot inside me, burning away everything all the way up through my chest and into my throat and I held on as long as I could, not for him anymore but for myself because I thought if I could just keep quiet, just let him keep lunging, keep pushing his fire up and into me, Jimmy Freeze might be able to burn me away to nothing . . .

. . . And then I wasn't just crying anymore but really freaking and that really freaked Jimmy too. He rolled off me real quick, like I'd electrocuted him down there or something, and I guess he just stood there next to the bed but I couldn't tell for sure because I couldn't stop screaming. I was wiggling way down under the covers and I kept screaming, "GET OUT! GET OUT!" and eventually he must have listened because I thought I could feel him not in the room anymore. I stopped screaming then but the crying just got worse until it felt like my heart was trapped inside my head and swelling and beating against the inside to get out. My head weighed a thousand throbbing pounds down under those covers and I wedged it as hard as I could into the space where the sheet and blanket folded around the mattress to keep my skull from flying apart. I never wanted to be dead like I wanted it then. Not even that night in the bathroom when Em found me, when it was more like the next step down into my hole than something I wanted to do. I could feel what it would be like to be dead, not to have to think about you or that day anymore or to live with what it's done to all of us. I could feel all the relief right along with the pain and the two mixed together into this warm thick buzz around my head like a gentle current of electricity. I stopped crying and curled myself into a ball down there, I mean really tight, with my nose between my knees, and the soft hum encircled my whole body and I was a baby in the womb. No, not even that. I was a single-celled creature floating alone in my own universe, not touching anyone or anything.

Then I felt a hand on my shoulder through the covers.

Jimmy hadn't gone anywhere. Or if he had he'd come back. And the way he was touching me, even though I couldn't see his face, I could tell he wouldn't leave, no matter what I said.

So that's when I told him about you. Everything.

And even though you already know, I need to tell you too. Because this isn't doing any good. You know that. If I were really fighting the silence of your death I'd be telling your story, not mine. So now I need to tell you because if I don't I know I'm going back into that hole again. Sometimes I am even angry at Em for being in the bathroom that night and for knowing something she couldn't have known, and I wonder if she knows the other thing, the thing Mom knows but would never tell, the thing you know but that I need to tell you anyway to not feel like I'm lying anymore. Because it's not enough that Mom is getting better if I'm not, if being at my Dad's is just hiding. I need to tell you about that day that still feels like today.

*I am supposed to be watching you.*

*I missed the bus again. Mom says to just wait, make myself use-ful. An hour later, you and I put Em on her bus and wave good-bye. The weather is perfect, still like summer, so I am chasing you around the yard, pretending to be a monster. You race and squeal, zig-zagging, The Big Z. We play until I can't run anymore. We sit on the steps a while to rest and talk. We talk all the time now, real conver-sations. Your diction is perfect except for a lisp I can see, your tongue darting out, perfectly pointed. A car pulls over and the driver says, Did we hear? Go tell your mother to turn on the television. Any sta-tion. You don't want to come in and you run behind the rhododen-dron, crouching, still playing the game. Stay right there.*

Inside, Mom is already watching, standing close to the tiny kitchen set rather than looking away long enough to move to the liv-ing room. I say, "What's happening," but she just stares so I do too. The towers are both smoking. Mom says, "Planes, two of them. One, then the other." Even on the tiny screen I think I can see some-

169

one falling. Then another. No, jumping. They're jumping from the tallest buildings in the world. Then we breathe in quick together as the first tower folds into the sidewalk. Mom says, "Oh God," asks where you are, a distracted afterthought, still looking. I don't hear her at first. My brain can't catch up with the reality of one hundred floors of people. She doesn't speak again, but the words suddenly reach me and I run back out of the house, down the steps, call that we need to go in. To you, I am starting the game again and you sprint, looking back at me, laughing, across the lawn, off the sidewalk, off the corner where the bus stopped every day for Em, and I swear to God, for the one and only time in my life, I can already see what is about to happen to you and what is going to happen to me because of it. I see it all in a split second before it even happens and then I watch it again. I watch you end your life and ruin mine. The car is moving fast, as if responding to the emergency playing in our kitchen. I expect an arm to come out of the window, put a blinking red light on the roof. I can see the driver as if I'm looking at him through binoculars, bending to adjust the volume on his radio, eyes wide at what he hears, which I can't understand because when he hits you there is only silence. My feet, pounding through the grass, make no sound. I know that my mouth is open, that air is rushing across my stretched vocal chords, but I hear nothing. You lift into the air and the car is past before you land silently at my feet, as if something as small as you couldn't possibly make a sound in a world where buildings can come down. It is a beautiful day so you are wearing a little orange sundress with a giraffe sewn on the front. The hem of the dress is at your thighs, right where it would be if you'd just laid down to pretend you were asleep. There is no blood. Your eyes are open but they don't move. Nothing moves, then your lips part.

*Following the ambulance, Mom's face is desperate from the short distance that separates her from you and she looks like she is trying hard not to drive right up and through the metal doors and into the bay next to the stretcher ten times the size of your body. "There was no blood, Mom. Mom, there was no blood." I keep telling her this, or trying to, as if it means something, no sound coming out. At the hospital, men and women in white roll you out, running, mouths moving to tell the others that run to meet them what your body is doing and not doing. We go through double doors like in a silent 3-D movie we have to run to keep seeing. I want to run the other way, back to the beginning now that I know what happens and pull you out. It feels like I can do this. Like nothing is real. The televisions hanging from the ceiling aimed at orange chairs show the airplanes going in, not coming out, disappearing like magic, special effects, repeated so many times I think I can figure out how they do it. Even the people pushing you look up as they pass. The first tower folds into the sidewalk, melting, like the Wicked Witch. First from the angle Mom and I saw in the kitchen. Then from another angle, and then another. It looks no more real than you look in the center of the white sheet, bouncing limp and silent as the front and then the back wheels cross a threshold, bump-bump, bump-bump. A woman squeezes a bag much smaller than the ones you see on TV and your little chest jumps all at once as if you've been surprised. We run between counters, nurses' stations, lines of people facing away, as if we are being shunned, all watching the planes knife in. And then you cross another threshold, bounce once, twice, bump-bump, bump-bump, and we are stopped while you continue. Mom fights the woman holding her, then gives up, falling into her, and we are led back through the backs of the others, more slowly now, and the planes, likewise, enter* slowly, perfectly swallowed, so that you don't even expect them to come out the other side.

Then we are in the orange chairs and four televisions are aimed at us. I look only not to think. Mom and I are alone. The only emergency in the world is on television. The second tower comes down. Again and again. Then time reverses and both stand in a perfect blue sky, just the kind of day you would choose to film this scene, and then it's the planes again, a new view of the second one now, from behind. All you see is the building, filling up the whole screen, and then the plane comes banking in from the left, flying away from you, entering dead center, right wing tipped above left, slicing an exact shape of itself, just a sliver of damage. But then the side view shows the exit wound, the ball of fire. Then tiny black grains of rice, falling. No. Jumping.

A doctor comes to find us too soon. It should take longer to save you. Mom starts to make a sound when she sees him. It is the first sound I have heard since you landed at my feet and I don't want to be hearing it. It is like the first sound of anguish a human being ever made. Her center of gravity contracts and her limbs are drawn inward. Impossibly, our mother's face is ugly. There was blood, lots of it, the doctor tells us. But on the inside. They did everything they could, the doctor says, trying not to look over Mom's shoulder at the television.

That is when David comes in, sees us and knows. And even more than wanting you alive, I want never to have known him so that he would never have to know me, never have taken me in and linked his life with mine just so this could happen. Without thinking to do it, I am crawling under the orange chairs when I feel his hand. "No no no," he says and draws us all together, heaving sorrow that pushes us apart, then back, like a pulse.

172

*The doctor is still there. Do we want to see you? They leave me with the doctor. I can't tell them I need to come. I see you going over the threshold, bump-bump, bump-bump, again and again. That's all I can see and I'm seeing it from different angles even though I only saw it from one. From one side I can see your head and limbs lift when the wheels hit the threshold. From the other side everything but the plastic tubing and your feet are blocked by the nurses' arms and I see that your right shoe is untied. From above, all the way from the ceiling, it looks like your little body gets two quick rhythmic shocks. Bump-bump, bump-bump. I make myself small inside the doctor's arm and try to slip under the orange chairs. "No no no," he says and pulls me into the curve of his neck and shoulder, rests his chin on my head, facing one of the televisions. I think I stay there with him a long time. He's not busy today.*

*When Mom comes back through the double doors, David holding her up, it's like he's bringing her back from a passageway to the future where she got old and will stay that way forever now. Her shoulders have rounded and her eyes look like she's blind. I know David is holding her because I can see his arm around her but I can't see his face. I don't ever want to see his face seeing me again.*

*I don't remember going home. No one knows what to do about Em so we do nothing. We let her come home on the school bus, race up the steps calling your name. There is something she wants to show you. She wants to know if you're up from your nap yet. My brain, not working, curled in the center of the circle of me on the couch, says no. She skips into the kitchen, Mom on the phone with Gram, crying, harder when Em appears. I hear the phone drop and Em's feet leave the floor.*

*My brain, encircled by the rest of me, is battling itself. Like when I started going to church and learned that you had to love God.*

In the night, my brain would say "I hate God" over and over, for no reason, just to test me, and I would force it to say "I love God," back and forth, until I was sure it had said more loves than hates, but then it would start all over again and become like counting sheep and when I woke in the morning I was never sure which side had won. Now my brain is saying, "I killed my sister," and I have no answer for that except for the wrong one which is that I hate you for it. I hate you. I love you. I hate you. God, sometimes I hate you so much. And I need for that to stop.

# Paper Doll

How many people like you died that day but not because of that day? I think about all those people. I think about some woman being interviewed for a job and she checks off the box that says "widow" and so someone asks her, when did her husband die?, and she says September 11, but then she knows she has to say something more, she has to say, But not in New York, not in Washington either, which feels, every time, like she's taking something away from him. Or I think about women lying in hospitals and giving birth on that day, pushing babies out into a world where things like that can happen, and I wonder when they hold their babies for the first time, does it feel so much different than it would have the day before? Or even people born in different years but on that date. Because that's what it is now—a day that's named after its date. Will those people ever be able to say I was born on September 11, without feeling like they have to look down and away at something off to the side when they say it?

And then there are the nightmares I have.

I have nightmares about all the blood. Yours and theirs. There are lines at the blood banks in New York five hours long, people desperate to open their veins. But they aren't pulling anyone out. All that blood for a few firefighters, enough to replace what seeped into the cavity of your little body thousands and thousands of times, gathered up and wasting away in big refrigerators hundreds of miles from us, dated like milk to be thrown away. Or maybe used for something else. Finger painting. I dream about finger painting with it, cold at first, then going warm at my touch, so much of it I don't have to conserve. I'm not stuck within eight and a half by eleven but can fling it against the white papered walls bucketfuls at a time. I can heave it up at the ceiling and let what doesn't stay there rain down on me, covering me. Then roll across the floor, *bump-bump*, *bump-bump*, a repeating print of myself trailing behind like an unfolded fan of paper dolls, lighter and lighter, until I disappear.

# Picture

When my Dad finally calls, Jimmy and I are asleep on my bed, curved around each other like quotation marks. We are both dressed, though I don't remember putting my clothes back on. The doctor says Frank was lucky. Since my Dad was already braking to stop in front of the house, the blow to his head looked worse than it was and didn't do any real damage. But when he went down the front tire rolled over his front leg and snapped it at the elbow, or whatever dogs have. He'll need surgery and be in a cast for at least six weeks. I tell Jimmy all of this as my Dad tells me, and I can feel the exhaustion of the day draining away and being replaced by a nervous energy that is almost magnetic. I ask my Dad a million questions he can't answer—when will Frank be home, will he be able to walk in his cast, what if he chews it right off, is he scared?—and I start pacing around the room while Jimmy sits up in my bed and watches me. My life seems to have sped up all of a sudden but I don't know where it's going and I have this sense that wherever it is, it's going there without me.

My Dad says he'll be home soon so Jimmy and I straighten up my room, spray some air freshener and sit out on the porch to wait. When the truck comes around the corner half an hour later, I realize we haven't said one word to each other.

"Hey," I say.

Jimmy looks up. "Hey."

"You okay?"

"Shouldn't I be asking you that?"

"I'm fine."

My Dad pulls slowly to the curb. He looks exhausted and it occurs to me that he probably hasn't slept in two days.

Jimmy says, "I feel like I took advantage of you or something."

"No. Don't think that. Nothing happened that I didn't want."

My Dad is coming around the front of the truck now. He's pulling the bunch of pink and white balloons behind him, some of which are losing helium and sagging out of the crowd.

"I do love you, Tess. I didn't say that just to . . ."

"I would never think that."

When my Dad is almost to the bottom of the steps he says, "What're you two whisperin' about?"

"Nothing, Dad."

He walks up the steps and right between us, as if there's no room on either side. "Well, I've had a shit stain of a day. I'm getting in the shower, then I'm goin' to bed. If you two wanna be together, here's your chance." He goes through the screen door and it slams behind him before he can get the balloons through.

He pulls at them and swears a couple times and then just lets them go up under the aluminum awning.

"Here's our chance," I say to Jimmy.

"Yep." He kisses me on the lips real soft and stands up to leave. "Will I see you at work tomorrow?"

"I think so."

"Okay."

He turns to go and I say, "Hey" to stop him.

"What?"

"While I'm telling you everything?"

"Yeah?"

"Do you remember that first time we talked? On these steps?"

"Sure."

"And I pretended I'd never seen you before?"

"Pretended?"

"I'd been watching you since like the day I got here."

"Yeah?"

"What about you?"

"What do you mean?"

"You know. Did you ever notice me?"

"What do you think?"

"I don't know. That's why I'm asking."

Jimmy shook his head. "Tess, when you're putting on all that makeup and looking at yourself, don't you ever really *look* at yourself?"

తం

It's late that night and I can't sleep. Frank's not with me but that's not it. My Dad is snoring loud enough from his room to register on the Richter scale but that's not it either. The problem is it's one A.M. and I'm not tired. Not even a little, and this nervous energy that started when my Dad called from the vet's has been building until I feel like I've had seventeen Mountain Dews and a two-pound bag of M&Ms. I've told Jimmy everything and that has made me feel free in a way I haven't for a very long time. But it's like I don't know what to do with that freedom. I'm just an atom bouncing off the walls of my Dad's house with no clear path other than where the next random bounce sends me.

Then finally I stop outside my Dad's room. The door is closed but it's the only place I haven't wandered yet. I know some kids who have OCD and the space behind my Dad's door has started to pull at me with the same force I imagine they feel when they haven't touched all the right things. Even though I know my Dad is in there the room starts to feel empty from me not paying attention to it. I've passed it four or five times—going from the kitchen for a snack I don't really want, back to my room to read a magazine I've read three times—until I finally stop and turn the knob and walk in and find what I've been looking for. Well, not exactly. But when I see the picture of my Mom and Dad on his dresser, I know I've been looking for you. I need to see you, a picture of you. I can't remember your face. I am so sure of what I need that I wake my Dad without even thinking that he needs sleep tonight more than what I need, because he couldn't. No one could need anything more than I need to see your face.

"Dad," I whisper.

He stops snoring.

"Daddy." I never call him that anymore and something about the way I say it wakes him right away.

"Tess, honey. What's the matter?" He says it softly, even though we are the only ones in the house.

"Daddy, I need to go home. I forgot something."

"What are you talking about?"

"I need to see her."

"Who?"

"Zoe."

"Sweetie, no. You're dreaming. Go back . . ."

"I didn't bring a picture of Zoe. I need to see a picture of Zoe."

"Oh. A picture. Okay. We'll get it in the morning."

"No, Daddy. I need to see it now."

"Now?"

"Right now."

He breathes deeply and lets out a long sigh. Then he pushes the covers back and rolls his feet to the floor, and the love I feel for him actually makes me dizzy and I have to grab his shoulder. He pats my arm with one hand and rubs his face with the other.

"We'll take the truck," he says, as if we have a choice.

# Home

The whole way to our house my Dad and I don't say anything.
If I didn't know him so well now I'd think he was mad at me.
But I can tell he's sad, even if I can't say exactly why.

When we get there and stop at the corner, I am looking at
our house for the first time since Em's last day of school. That's
weird enough by itself, but sitting in my Dad's truck at two
o'clock in the morning and fingering my back-door key makes
everything feel like a dream. The house is dark, so dark it looks
too heavy for the ground it's sitting on, all softened up with
dew. For a couple minutes I can't move so I make myself believe our house could sink into the swampy yard if I don't get
out and touch it and make it real again.

"I'll be right back, Dad."

"I'll be here."

For some reason I feel like I need to stay hidden so I take
the narrow path between our house and the one next door instead of walking around through the front and side yards. At

least I remember the path being narrow. But now when I look up I can see it would be impossible to climb from Em's window into our neighbor's house. We are separated by just enough space to have our own lives. I drag my hand along the brick and it feels cool and hard and very real.

I move fast because if I don't I'll turn around and go back. Around the corner, past the garbage cans, up onto the back stoop, through the door, into the laundry room and through the kitchen. I've never been away long enough to really notice that our house has a smell, but as soon as I reach the dining room I realize I would know I was home with my eyes closed. It's hard to describe but you'd know it too, sort of old carpet and lemon and Mom's shampoo all mixed together and softened.

I was worried about being able to see but I shouldn't have been. If you remember, our house is real big and old and there are windows everywhere facing the street corner. It's almost like being outside so light's not a problem. There are pictures on the walls and on the tables, some of you, I can feel them, but they're not the one I'm looking for. In this light I'd have to get right up close and then try to keep remembering, which I don't trust myself to do. I need something I can carry with me and look at whenever I want, like Jimmy does with his mom.

The creaky hardwood floors start in the dining room. I try to step from one oriental rug to the next to stay quiet, through the living room and the front hall to the bottom of the staircase. All around the front door there are these old leaded-glass windows that make designs on the floor out of the streetlights. It's like walking on water in the moonlight. I keep away from the banister, close to the wall, going up the stairs because they creak less on that side. It gets dark for a minute when I reach the first landing, but when I turn the corner I can see by the night-light Mom leaves on so Em can find her way to the bathroom in the night.

Your room is the first one at the top of the stairs. When I look in, I see that both the crib and the little bed are gone. There's a tall bed in there now that looks like an antique, with four long posters and a flowered quilt. Mom has stenciled flowers around the wall up near the ceiling and there's a tall, thin lamp with a flowered shade that sits on a nightstand next to the bed. The night-light from the hall doesn't reach all the way back to the far corner but there is a big piece of furniture there, like an armoire or something. I remember the day Mom painted in there and how that made me feel so lonely, like she was betraying both of us somehow, but I don't feel that way looking at your room now. I'm not sure why. What it does though is make me feel for a minute like I'm not in my own house, so when I leave your room and peek into my own next door, it's with the feeling that someone else could be living in there now.

My room faces the sidewalk where my Dad is parked and the blinds are all up, so everything in my room glows from the streetlights. I don't know what I was expecting but I am surprised to see that nothing has changed. I still have the same bed, the same comforter, the same desk and lamp with the green shade. My magazines are still stacked on the bottom shelf of my bookcase and pictures of my friends are still stuck all around in the frame of the mirror above my dresser. There's an empty space, though. One picture is missing and of course it's the one I'm looking for. I know exactly where it is almost before I realize it's gone, but I don't want to wake Em and then leave her again. For a minute I feel lost in my own room. Then I remember something else. I go to the front window and see the truck sitting at the curb before pulling the blind and making it disappear. Then I pull the other two blinds and shut the door quietly. I close my eyes as tight as I can, turn on the light and count to fifty. When I turn the light back off, I keep my eyes closed and feel my way to my bed and lie down on my back. Then I open my eyes and look up. The stars have come out on my ceiling. All the constellations are still there—the Big Dipper, Cassiopeia, Leo, Orion. I can see the Seven Sisters and Gemini and Cepheus and Draco the Dragon winding his way through all of them. I don't even realize I'm crying until a tear kind of tickles one of my ears, and then I know why my Dad is sad. It's because as usual I am the last person to know what's going to happen to me. Somehow, he already knows I'm not going back with him.

The night-light in the hall gives off just enough light for me to read the sign on Em's door. It's a piece of cardboard from one of David's work shirts and there is pink crepe paper around the border and it says:

Apartment 1-A
EMILY ELIZABETH GLADSTONE
<u>No Soliciting</u>

I turn her doorknob as quietly as I can and walk in.

She is asleep, curled on her side. Her thin hair is across her face and she doesn't move even after I sit down on her bed. When I tuck her hair behind her ear, she opens her eyes and looks at me like I am exactly who she expected to see.

She says, "Hey, Tess," already wide awake.

"Hey."

"Are you home?"

"Yeah."

"Are you staying?"

"Yeah."

"That's good."

She rolls onto her back, stretches her arms and then folds her hands behind her head like we're chatting at a slumber party. The silent treatment I got at Kennywood was nothing more than that. This was all I had to do to make things right between us.

"Did you see the card I made for you?"

"No."

"It's down on the counter in the kitchen. It's pretty good."

"I'm sure it is."

"Mom said we should probably send it, but I said if I didn't see you on your birthday I'd be seeing you when school starts. School starts Monday, you know."

"I know."

"Is that why you're back?"

"No."

She thinks about that for a minute and seems satisfied with my answer.

"Miss Ellenbogen moved to Ohio. I'm going to have Mrs. Gumpto."

"I know. Mom told me. Is she supposed to be nice?"

"I think so. Madison Root had her last year and she said the skin under her arm wobbles all over the place when she writes on the board."

"That's not so bad."

"And she smells like cough drops all the time."

"Not everyone can be Miss Ellenbogen."

"But Madison said she's nice."

"That's good."

Em sits up now and pulls her knees up to her chest, then pulls her nightgown tight over her knees and tucks it under her feet.

"Who do you have?" she asks.

"What do you mean?"

"For school. Who's your teacher this year?"

"When you get older you don't have just one. You have different ones for every class."

"I wouldn't like that."

"It's not so bad."

"I like to get to know someone."

"You get used to it."

"I guess."

Em seems to have that same nervous energy I had earlier and I know she'd sit and talk like this all night. But my Dad is waiting for me to tell him what I'm going to do.

"Hey, Em?"

"Yeah?"

"You know that picture I had in my mirror? The one of Zoe?"

"Yeah."

"Do you know where it is?"

"I'm real careful with it."

"I know. I just need it back for a while."

"Okay."

She slides her knees out from under her nightgown and

rolls over onto them. Then she reaches her arm up under her pillow and pulls it out.

"Here."

I can't even look at the picture because I can't look away from Em's face.

"Put it back," I say.

"But you can have it. I don't need it anymore."

"No. Put it back. I'll borrow it tomorrow. You sleep with it tonight."

"You sleep with me then."

She tucks the picture back into its hiding place and lies down on her back with her head just barely touching the pillow, making room for me.

"Come on, lie down. My bed's real comfortable."

"I have to go tell my Dad something first."

"Nick's here?"

"He brought me."

"You still can't drive?"

"No. Not yet. Hey, I'll be right back, okay?"

"Okay."

I get up to leave but turn back to her when I reach the door.

"Hey, Em?"

"Yeah?"

"What's up with the sign?"

"I made it."

"Do you know what 'no soliciting' means?"

"Yeah. We had to learn it for Brownies."

"But why do you need it for your room?"

"I don't know. Just in case."

That makes me want to cry again for some reason, but not in a sad way, and I leave the room before Em can see me.

∽

Walking up to the truck, I don't know what I'm going to say. My Dad is slouched down in his seat with his chin on his chest, breathing heavily. He wakes up when I climb in and looks at me. Then he nods and looks at the steering wheel. I still can't say anything so he says, "I'll bring your stuff tomorrow."

"I'm sorry, Dad."

"What for? I never thought you were stayin' forever."

"Really?"

"With me? Naw."

He looks back at the steering wheel and pushes against it, stretching out his thick arms. "What about Frank?" he says.

"What do you mean?"

"Do you think your Mom'd let you?"

"Keep him?"

"He's your dog, Tess."

I hug him real hard and he pulls me into his lap and we sit like that for a minute, with my head under his chin. Then he says I better go before he decides to kidnap me for the rest of my life, so I do. I am standing alone on the sidewalk, and when he starts the truck I expect every light in the neighborhood to go on from the noise. He forces it into gear and there's even more noise and he says something I don't hear.

"What, Dad?"

He shouts. "I said, happy birthday!" Then he smiles and waves and pulls away.

When I turn around I can't help standing and just looking at our house. It's not sinking anymore. It's big and solid and I can't even take it all in at once so I look at it in pieces, letting it fill me up. When my eyes get to my own window there is an outline of Emily there, but only for a second. She doesn't wave or try to get my attention. I think she's just making sure I'm not leaving, that I'm really home. Once my Dad's truck is out of sight, she disappears too.

I'm not sure why but I stand a while longer, looking up at my empty window. And I keep standing there until all of a sudden I feel like I can't move and I don't know why until I look down and right there in front of me is the spot in the grass where you landed at my feet. There's nothing that marks it or makes it different, not even a bare patch in the grass, but I know it anyway, and for a few seconds everything goes quiet again, like when it happened, and all I can hear is the blood pumping in my head, which is getting louder and louder. Before I even know what I'm doing I am taking off my shoes and socks and stepping with one foot and then the other right onto that spot. And then there is sound and I can hear everything. Standing there with my feet together and my arms at my sides and my shadow from the streetlight stretching across the lawn toward our house, I can hear the leaves in the trees and wind chimes from the house next door and the summer insects and myself crying but only softly. I can hear a car a few streets down stopping at a stop sign then starting down the next block and when that sound has faded away I can even hear the hum from the streetlight on the corner. The grass is long and needs to be cut. I lift one bare foot and wave it back and forth in front of me across the tops of the grass and I can hear the swishing sound your feet used to make when I would swing you there. I keep doing that, back and forth, *swish-swish*, until I hear something else, and I look up to see Em back at my window, tapping softly to tell me it's time to come in.

Mom cried real hard when she came into Em's room the next morning. David had already left for work but when he came home he gave me one of his best I-love-you-like-you're-my-own hugs, which I know he means. So far we're doing okay. We all go to see the doctor together, even Em, so I guess that's something, a start. David didn't want her to go but I said I wouldn't come otherwise. She mostly just listens. She doesn't cry when we do, which is pretty often, but she's sharing our grief in some way and that's what's important. Sometimes I think she's lucky being so young because she'll forget easier. But then she'll be playing dolls all by herself and she'll start to cry real quietly.

I'm busy with school and everything so I don't see my Dad much more than I used to, but we talk all the time and there's something between us that wasn't there before we lived together. He knows me now, and I know him. One thing we do that we didn't do much before is every other Sunday we go to church together. I sit between my Dad and Gram, and Mo Mo is always with us too. I stay with her when Dad and Gram go up for Communion and when one of the young priests walks back to serve her, she reaches her bony hand over to my leg and lays it there as if to include me.

My Dad brought Frank over about a week after he dropped me off and Frank got about as excited as he could get considering his condition. He has a cast on his front right leg and one of those big white cone things around his neck to keep him from chewing it off. He looks like that little RCA dog except instead of peeking into the phonograph speaker he's peeking out of it, all curious about how he got in there. He and Em already love each other, and sometimes Frank even sleeps with her instead of me.

I see Jimmy all the time. He still doesn't have a driver's license but my Dad lets him borrow the truck anyway. We go to the movies or bowling or just hang around our house. He thinks Mom is gorgeous, of course. We're back to kissing a lot but we haven't had sex again. We both agreed it wasn't such a good idea right now. I don't usually make a big deal out of what words people choose to use to express themselves. I mean my vocabulary is the pits so I'm not one to talk. But it always made me angry, even before, when girls would say they *lost* their virginity. It sounds so careless, like it was something they couldn't keep track of. But I don't know how to do any better because there *is* a loss that happens. It's not just the virginity that's lost, it's something else, something less obvious but more important, something you can't even identify really because you never knew you had it to lose. Innocence is too easy. It's more than that. It's more like you lose part of that feeling that there are things out there waiting for you. Because you've been waiting for it and fearing it and wanting it, and when it finally happens, you find out it's a physical act that begins and ends, and you're mostly sorry to have learned that. It doesn't mysteriously make you a woman. It just makes you a girl who's done it. If there's a word for that, I don't know it yet.

Sometimes at the doctor's we talk about how we are all numb to the videos—of the planes hitting the buildings, of the buildings coming down—not just now but always, how we never felt the way everyone else did that day. That "we" was one of the most important things for me, to find out Mom and David felt the same way, and then to understand that even we weren't alone. That on any day you could pick there are thousands and thousands of little deaths, tiny tragedies, and that all of them matter.

On the anniversary Mom and David and Em and I are going to stay home all day with no TV, no radio, nothing from the outside world. We're going to watch home videos of all of us, look at photo albums, talk about you and remember you all day while the world is remembering everyone else. We'll probably cry a lot but we'll laugh too. No one could watch you or look at pictures of you without laughing even if they tried. I've been carrying around the picture Em had ever since I came home, and it's already getting a little smudged and crinkled around the edges from the number of times I take it out of its plastic slip. I don't know why I have to take it out but it feels like I can't see you all the way if I don't, like I'm looking at it in a dream through the plastic. You're sitting on that rope swing you loved at the park, the one that's all by itself, away from the big swing set and the slides, and you're wearing that polka dot skirt with the frilly edge you loved to twirl around in. It makes me feel good to look at it. Not just better, but really good. Even though you're the only one in the picture it feels like we're all there. I remember Mom had the camera and David was behind her, trying to get you to look at them, but you kept looking over your shoulder at Em and me, laughing at the faces we were making, and that's what you're doing in the picture, your eyes so shiny I feel like I could see all of us reflected in them if I could just get close enough. You can't even see the tree that the rope's hanging from so it looks like it just goes up and up forever, and your hands are clasped around it so tight that I can almost feel the force of your grip in the pink and white of your little knuckles, squeezing life up the rope and into the sky.

Remember how I said nothing changes everything? I think I was wrong about that. I'm starting to think maybe everything changes everything. That we never know what's going to happen next and we're not even supposed to. Maybe "Z" is the shape of everyone's life. You're going along in what feels like a straight line, headed for one horizon, the only one as far as you know, and then something happens, maybe something good, maybe something terrible, or maybe just something like seeing a guy picking out a cantaloupe at the store, something that feels like nothing, and all of a sudden you're headed at another horizon altogether. Good things can happen that you did nothing to deserve. Bad things can happen that aren't really anyone's fault. And it's sad how, if you let yourself, it's so much easier to think about what you've lost instead of what you have left. I'm not saying everything's okay, because it's not. We will never, ever be the same without you. We have our good and bad days as a family, and you will always be the invisible center of both. But love is this really powerful thing that everyone's got if they'd just learn how to accept it. I mean, come on. If it's something we all have to give, and if it's something we all want, doesn't that mean there's exactly enough to go around?

Love Always,

*Jess*

## Acknowledgments

My profound gratitude for varying reasons (but in unvarying degree) to Melinda and Philip Beard, Sr., John Towle, Jane Dystel, Miriam Goderich, Amy King, Eric Kampmann, Maryglenn McCombs, Jason Gobble, Clare Ferraro, Carolyn Carlson, Laura Hilgers, Scott Gelotti, Fred Busch, Buddy Nordan, Dan Jones, Mark Schoeppner, Stan Druckenmiller, Seth Tobias, and everyone at the law firm of Stonecipher, Cunningham, Beard and Schmitt. Each of you has made this book better, or possible, or both. That said, there is only one person without whom Tess's story could never have been told. Traci: I know you signed up for a confident, young lawyer and not some vulnerable, fortysomething dreamer who follows his fortune cookie future; but, impossibly, the latter loves you even more than the former did.

—PB